MONKEY ISLAND

Paula Fox

ORCHARD BOOKS

ORCHARD BOOKS
96 Leonard Street, London EC2A 4RH
Orchard Books Australia
14 Mars Road, Lane Cove, NSW 2066
ISBN 1 85213 853 X (paperback)
ISBN 1 85213 392 9 (hardback)
Originally published in the United States in 1991
as a Richard Jackson Book by Orchard Books
First published in Great Britain 1992
First paperback publication 1995
Text copyright © Paula Fox 1992
A CIP catalogue record for this book is available from the British Library.
Printed in Great Britain

*For Andrew Lee Sigerson
and his dear mother, Kathleen*

Contents

1 The Hotel

Clay Garrity's mother, Angela, had been gone five days from the room in the hotel where they had been living since the middle of October.

On the first evening of her disappearance, he'd waited until long past dark before going to a small table that held a hot plate, a few pieces of china, two glasses, and some cutlery as well as their food supply: a jar of peanut butter, half a loaf of bread in a plastic sack, some bananas, a can of vegetable soup, and a box of doughnuts.

His mother usually heated soup for their supper and made hot cereal for his breakfast in the pot that sat on the hot plate. Clay lifted the lid. There was nothing inside. During their first week in the hotel, she had made a stew that lasted them for three days. That was the only time she had really cooked.

He ate a banana, then picked up the box of doughnuts. Beneath it, he found twenty-eight dollars and three quarters.

He wasn't especially worried yet about her not coming home. She'd been gone entire days before, not returning until nightfall. But the sight of the money made him uneasy.

Why had she left it there, almost hidden, as if she meant for him to find it after she'd gone? Could she have forgotten it? Where would you go in New York City without money? Still, she might have put the twenty-eight dollars aside for something special, like the clinic where she went for check-ups, or for the new shoes she said he would soon need. The quarters could have been for making phone calls. And she might have had more money in her pocketbook. But he couldn't quite believe that, because she hardly ever had more than twenty-five dollars after buying their groceries.

He ate half of a doughnut as he stood at the table, staring at the carton of milk that stood outside on the sill of one of the room's two windows. He thought of pouring himself a glass, but, in a flash, he didn't want it at all. Even the rest of the doughnut felt too thick to go down his throat.

He took the only chair in the room, straight backed and painted with a colour his mother called down-and-out brown, to the other window and sat there a while, looking at the street five storeys below. The traffic was light at this hour. Most of the people who drove past the hotel on their way to the tunnels that went to New Jersey had gone home by now.

Clay imagined a tunnel going under the Hudson River, imagined the dark, moving water above it and beneath it, people in their cars who talked and listened to their radios that must crackle at such a depth, under so much water and earth and concrete.

On the floor beside his mother's bed was a small, battery-run radio. In the mornings while he was getting ready for school, washing his face at the basin and dressing, his mother would listen to a news programme. Lately, she had been turning the radio on as soon as she came into the room, even before taking off her coat and putting down the bag of groceries she was carrying. When he did his homework, she lowered the volume. But she seemed to want some kind of sound all the time and didn't care whether it was music or people talking.

Once when he awoke in the night, needing to go to the bathroom, which was outside the room and down at the end of the long corridor near the stairs, he saw her lying in bed, holding the radio on her chest, its dial face casting a pale glow on her chin and mouth, a faint babbling noise issuing from it like voices in a distant room.

"Be careful," she murmured as he went to the door, his key in his hand. He knew that; he knew you always had to be careful when you went outside the room.

He sat absolutely still, his gaze fixed now on the big apartment building across the street through whose windows he could see people moving about in lighted rooms among large potted plants. In the old life, in the apartment where they had once lived with his father, they had had two pots of African violets, and when

11

one of the deep mauve flowers bloomed, it seemed to fill his mother with delight.

The stillness that had come over him was almost like sleep. It was abruptly broken by an urge to look behind him. The first thing his turning glance fell upon was the wheeled metal rack they had found in the room when they moved into the hotel a month ago, and from which their clothes hung. His mother had told him that when people gave parties, they rented such racks for guests to hang their coats on. Probably the rack was left over from the days when the hotel was a real hotel, not an ants' nest of ugly rooms where people in trouble waited for something better—or worse—to happen to them.

What he saw, hanging from a wire hanger, was his mother's brown wool coat. He placed his hand against the windowpane. It was cold, like the door of a refrigerator. Where would she have gone? Without her coat?

Soon, he would have to go out to the corridor and to the bathroom that was used by nearly everyone on the floor, though he'd heard there was one room that had its own toilet and tub instead of just a washbasin. He would have to lock the door and hope there were no people leaning against the walls, people who would watch his every step as he went towards a battered door you couldn't lock, and into the bathroom with its tub full of fans of tobacco-coloured stains, the toilet sweating moisture.

But he couldn't go to the bathroom right now, though he needed to. He took a book from a cardboard box that also held some old stubby crayons and a Lego set he no longer played with. Then he pulled his mother's coat off its hanger. He got onto his cot and covered himself with most of it, drew up his legs, and turned the pages of *Robinson Crusoe* to the place where he had stopped reading yesterday. The words he glanced at made no sense at all. He lay there, his finger in the book, the coat collar against his cheek. He was eleven years old, and he had never felt so alone in his life.

Clay didn't go to school in the morning and not for the rest of the week either.

During the days, he wandered along the hotel corridors and up and down the grey cement stairways. He was always cautious, on the lookout for older boys and girls, some of whom would take whatever you were carrying away from you, and even your clothes. From behind locked doors of rooms, he heard people talking or quarrelling. He heard loud radios playing what his mother called "hammer music", and sometimes children laughing and shouting or crying.

There was supposed to be a security man in the lobby, but he seldom showed up. Still, when Clay walked through there, he felt nervous. If the security man suddenly appeared, he'd ask Clay why he wasn't in school. He might call the police.

One morning he went to a park several blocks east. The only children in the play area were babies in strollers or carriages wheeled by their mothers, and there was nothing to do but watch them. A policeman came and stood behind the swings to smoke a cigarette. Clay left at once.

There was nothing to do on the street near the hotel either except watch the passing cars, or the people going in and out of the apartment house across the street. He wasn't worried about their noticing him. They never looked at the hotel. They didn't look at much except the dogs some of them led on leashes out to the sidewalk at dusk.

At night he didn't get under the blanket on his cot but slept beneath his mother's coat. He had eaten the bread, the bananas, and the doughnuts. Although he was hungry, he didn't open the can of soup and heat it up. The thought came to him that it was his mother who should do that, who should turn on the hot plate and open the can with the opener she had bought at the little hardware store around the corner. If he opened the can of soup, she wouldn't come back.

But he knew he had to eat, even though something peculiar had happened to his appetite. It was as if all the hunger he felt was only in his head, not in his stomach. On the third night he'd been alone, he opened the door a crack and waited for Mrs. Larkin, who lived in the next room with her backward son, Jacob, to put out her garbage in a black plastic bag.

During the night, someone was supposed to collect the garbage people left outside their doors even though that was against the hotel rules. There was always enough left scattered along the corridor to sour the air.

He waited for what seemed an hour until he heard Mrs. Larkin drop the bag on the floor and lock her door. He tiptoed out and went to the bag and undid the thick, slippery knot. He found a few pieces of bread, a chicken wing that had a little meat left on it and which he ate with a slight shudder, and an apple with one bite taken from it. His mother had told him that Jacob didn't like anything but french fries, and Mrs. Larkin had to throw away most of the food she tried to persuade him to eat.

As Clay lay in bed, his hands gripping the coat, he knew something was bound to happen. Someone would come to the room, maybe two or three people. The school might send a truant officer. The woman his mother called Miss You-can't-fool-me would turn up from Social Services, or else the man from Missing Persons, who always wore a whole suit and who had visited them twice before in their old apartment, would step into the room, his mouth full of questions about Clay's father: Did Mr. Garrity drink? Take drugs? Had he been depressed? Was he unstable? Was Mrs. Garrity sure he wasn't living somewhere with another wife? His mother had said, as she gave the man a photograph of his father, "He's been out of work a long time."

For as far back as Clay could recall, his father had gone to his office carrying a large leather portfolio that held layouts for the magazine where he was the art director. Not much art, his father often said. It was more like being a puzzle director, figuring out how the copy would fit around the advertising and the photographs. Then the magazine folded. That is, his father explained to him, it ran out of subscribers and money.

Mr. Garrity began to collect unemployment insurance and look for the same kind of job he had lost. But it seemed that many magazines were folding and many art directors were looking for work and not finding it. After a few months, he was hired by a house painter and painted apartments all over the city. Then the painter fell ill and went back to Greece, where he had come from, and where his family could help take care of him. Mr. Garrity sold ties for a few weeks in a men's clothing store and took his lunch to work in a paper bag to save money. But the manager of the store said Mr. Garrity wasn't friendly enough to customers and wasn't cut out to be a salesman.

He kept looking for work, any kind of work. And then one morning he said he couldn't go out their front door, he had to think, he had to figure out what had happened to his life.

Clay's mother was afraid of the doorbell ringing. It might be a bill collector or someone from the landlord's office. "Something has to be done," she had said. His father had not looked up at her words but continued to stare at his shoes, which, Clay had noticed, were dusty and worn down at the heels.

One evening his mother came home an hour after the time when they usually sat down to supper. Her face was flushed as though she'd been running, and her voice, which was usually low and agreeable, was loud and sharp. She had gone to see an old school friend, she said. "You remember Maggie?" she asked. Mr. Garrity nodded, not looking interested. "She's made a lot of money designing sports clothes and she's loaned me—it's strictly a loan, Lawrence—enough money so I can enrol in a computer course and take care of things while I'm being trained. There are jobs out there, and I'm going to get one of them."

Clay had been doing his homework on the kitchen table and, after a minute or two, he looked up at his mother and father because neither of them was saying a word. He saw a look pass between them that startled him. It was as if they had never met each other before. His father pressed himself back in the chair he was sitting in, drawing in his elbows and legs. His mother stood a few feet away, her face still red, one arm held out, her palm turned up as though she was offering him something.

His mother completed her course and found a job in a Wall Street office, where she worked what she called the graveyard shift, from eleven to seven in the morning. "All alone up there on the thirty-fifth floor with machines humming and clicking away," she said.

"I sort of like it." When she came home, Clay was usually on his way to school, not the one he'd been going to since they'd had to move into the hotel.

The flush faded away from his mother's face, and her voice lost its sharpness. The rent was paid, and some early evenings the three of them even went out to supper at a Chinese restaurant in the neighbourhood, where they had gone often when his father was still an art director. But something was different.

Whatever it was, it always began around supper-time. They would all be in the kitchen, his father looking down at the stove at something he'd cooked—he did most of the cooking now—and his mother might be at the sink, washing lettuce. Whatever it was didn't show itself in words. It was hidden somewhere in the hot silence.

Clay tried to ignore it while he was eating supper. But he thought about it in school. "You're not paying attention, Clay," his homeroom teacher said. "You're daydreaming."

He wasn't daydreaming, he wanted to protest. He was thinking so hard his forehead ached.

One night loud voices from the living room woke him. His mother and father were fighting.

"How *can* we?" his father suddenly shouted. "I might never get work again except for piddling temporary jobs. Another baby? You're crazy!"

"It's too late now," his mother cried out. "We'll have to find a way."

Clay pulled the covers over his head, then reached out and pushed the pillow on top of the covers.

The next day, his father met him after school and took him to the zoo. It was rainy, and most of the animals had retreated into the sheltered areas of their cages. Only a tiger paced behind the bars, panting, its golden eyes passing over their faces as though they were stones, its great paws slapping the wet cement floor of its cage.

"I think the tiger hates being in there," his father said.

"It gets fed," Clay said.

"That's true. Just enough food so it will have the energy to pace."

Clay did not feel his father was speaking to him; he might even have forgotten that Clay was there, standing next to him.

Clay's mother was put on an earlier shift for a week, so Mr. Garrity and Clay were alone in the kitchen in the evening. At first Clay felt relieved by a kind of calm silence between them as they both went about fixing their supper. But when his father didn't say a word while they were eating their hamburgers and baked potatoes, Clay made up a story about a lost dog following him home, because he wanted to hear a voice, even if it was just his own.

His father kept his head bowed over his plate. Was he listening? At last Clay said, "Daddy? Could you say something?"

His father stood up so quickly his chair fell to the floor with a bang. He came quickly to Clay's side and crouched down and put his arms around him tightly. Clay could barely breathe. "I'm sorry," his father said over and over again.

Later, when he leaned down to kiss Clay goodnight before turning off the light on the table next to the bed, he took a five dollar bill from his jacket pocket and tucked it under the pillow. "That's for you to buy something nice tomorrow," he said. "Maybe that ring puzzle you liked that we saw yesterday in the stationery store."

Stationery store. Those were the last words he heard from his father. He was gone the next morning, and he didn't come back.

People came to the apartment—a colleague of his father's from the magazine that had folded; Maggie, his mother's rich friend; their next-door neighbours, a couple whom they hadn't seen much of since his father had lost his job; and finally the man from Missing Persons, who came twice.

His mother continued to go to work at night. She had to, she told Clay. You can't live in a place like this without money, she said.

She gave a key to the neighbour woman to look in on him during the night. Clay wondered if it was his father's key. Most mornings she managed to get home in time to make him breakfast. In school, he thought of her sleeping in the broad daylight while the cars honked on the street below their windows.

There was no word from his father. "Is he dead?" Clay asked one evening.

"I think he's looking for work," his mother said. "I'm sure he's going to find a job so he can take care of us and . . . the new baby." She glanced at him. "You don't look surprised," she said.

"I heard you one night," he said. "I heard about the baby."

She looked away from him, her hands gripped in her lap. "I'm sorry you heard about it that way," she said.

Not more than a few weeks after that conversation, his mother had to stop work. The doctor said she might lose the baby if she kept on the way she was going, working too hard and not getting enough sleep. During the days she went out, "to get help," she told Clay. That's when he first heard about Social Services and aid for dependent mothers and minors. He was a minor because of his age.

He thought of himself as another kind of miner, one who went deep into dark, airless passages beneath mountains, searching for something.

Now he kept moving during daylight. He didn't think about much except making himself invisible so that the security guard, the teenagers who hung out in the corridors and stairwell, and the people who gathered in clumps in the lobby during the afternoons and evenings wouldn't notice him at all.

On the fifth night that his mother didn't return, he had just gotten the knot undone on Mrs. Larkin's plastic bag when she suddenly opened the door. He gasped.

"Take it easy," Mrs. Larkin said. Clay glimpsed Jacob sitting on a bed, watching the screen of a small television set with the sound turned off, his feet turned out like a duck's feet.

"What's going on here?" Mrs. Larkin asked. She reached out and grabbed Clay's hand. "Where's your mother?"

He couldn't answer. His throat had closed up.

"I wondered who'd been going through my garbage," she was saying. He realised from her voice that she wasn't going to be angry.

"She went away to look for my father," he managed to say, but his words ran together and he wasn't sure, from watching her face, that she'd understood him. She was still holding his hand, but her grip loosened. He could have pulled away. For the moment, he didn't want to.

"Come on in," she said. "I'm going to give you a bit of supper, late as it is, and you're going to tell me what's up."

Jacob slowly turned his head to look at Clay. He was a grown-up man, but Clay knew that his body and head were only a costume. He didn't see or hear too well. He often moaned like a seal. But he could smile, and he smiled now at Clay and waved at him with one of his big lumpy hands that was like a work glove full of sand.

"That's right, Jacob," Mrs. Larkin said. "Wave to him so's he'll know he's welcome."

There was a real stove in the room, although it was very small, like a toy stove, and Mrs. Larkin towered over it. Soon she had filled a bowl with pea soup and put it on a little table, along with a spoon and two pieces of dark bread covered with margarine. She took a chair to the table and said to Clay, "Go to it."

As he looked at the food, Clay was afraid he might shout with the hunger he suddenly felt and that had been, somehow, postponed until this very minute. He ate everything. When he'd finished, he looked up to see that Jacob had fallen over on his side and was moaning. Mrs. Larkin took hold of his shoulders and set him upright as though he was a big doll.

She turned to Clay. "Tell me," she said.

"She didn't come back," he said.

"Since when?"

"Five days," he answered.

"You've been alone all this time?" she asked.

He nodded.

"Did you go to school every day?"

He shook his head.

Mrs. Larkin gripped her hands together.

"Clay, I think we have to do something about this. You know, your mother's going to have a baby. She shouldn't be out there . . . wandering the streets."

A shaft of fear went through him. Like his hunger, the fear had been postponed until now. The two people he knew best in the world, who knew him best, were gone, hidden somewhere in the vast city.

He guessed Mrs. Larkin would get hold of someone like Miss You-can't-fool-me, and she would ask him questions he couldn't answer. Or worse, a policeman would take him to an unknown place, and when his mother came back, he'd be gone. Then all three of them would be lost to one another.

"She'll be back," he said in a whisper.

"In the morning, I'll make some phone calls," Mrs. Larkin said. She was staring hard at him and she must have seen the fear he felt. "There have to be phone calls," she said, and reached out to pat his shoulder.

"She's gone away before," he said quickly. "And I've got food. I just didn't eat it because . . . there was a lost dog in the stairwell and I gave it to him." That dog again, he thought, remembering the story he'd made up to tell his father. His alibi dog.

Mrs. Larkin went to adjust a pillow behind Jacob's back, and he suddenly flung his arms around her and hid his face in her neck.

"There, there . . ." she said absently, stroking his thin, stiff hair.

After a moment, she turned back to Clay. "You'll have to be alone tonight," she said. "Unless you'd like to bring in a blanket and sleep on the floor? You're welcome to do that, but Jacob makes a fearsome

24

amount of noise at night and it would keep you awake." She looked at Clay silently. Then, as though she'd made up her mind, she said firmly, "No, I won't wait till morning. I ought to do it now. You could watch Jacob for me, and I'll go down to the lobby and call the police to tell them your mama is missing."

"She isn't missing," Clay protested. Why had he been so stupid as to tell her about the five days?

"Yes, I'll do that," Mrs. Larkin said. "It might take a while if there's a lot of people lined up for the phone. But it's late, so maybe there won't be. It's awful you've been by yourself with all the trash doing their nasty things all over this place."

"All right, I'll watch Jacob," Clay said, feeling his breath coming fast. "But I'd like to get a book I'm reading from my room. I'll come right back."

"Okay, Clay," she said.

He could see she believed him and he felt bad about what he was going to do, almost as bad as he felt about the fear and uncertainty of it.

He went next door to the room. On the rack, next to the white blouse and blue skirt his mother wore when she had to go to agencies and sign papers so they could get help, was his beige corduroy jacket. He had never worn it around the hotel, because someone would have taken it from him. Next to the jacket, hanging by a loop on a hanger, was his old down jacket. He could hardly get into it any more, it was so tight, and he decided to leave it there. In one of the two suitcases where he kept his clothes, he found a cotton shirt and a necktie he hadn't worn since the Christmas pro-gramme at school last December. That was before his father had lost his job, before everything had hap-pened. He put on the shirt hurriedly but dropped the tie back in the suitcase. Then he remembered the twenty-eight dollars and the three quarters, and he stuffed the money in a pocket of the jacket.

He heard footsteps in the corridor and he peeked out the door and saw Mrs. Larkin leading Jacob towards the bathroom, both of them looking down at Jacob's slow-moving feet. Clay glanced around the room. You could hardly tell anyone had been living in it except for the two suitcases, a box of books, the few clothes on the rack, and his mother's rumpled coat on his cot.

He made sure his key was pinned to the inside of his pants pocket before he opened the door. He could have taken the elevator, which was in the opposite direction from the bathroom, but even in the daytime he and his mother seldom used it. "A poison box," she had called it. You could get caught in it with someone who might do something terrible to you. Sometimes the elevator stopped between floors, and you'd have to stay there an hour until it was fixed, reading all the things people had written on the four walls, even on the ceiling.

He went to the stairs and looked down. He didn't like them, although you had a chance to escape, which you didn't have if you were in the elevator. Often there were big kids leaning against the railings smoking dope. But as he made his way down cautiously to the lobby, he passed only one old woman carrying a greasy bag from the fast-food ribs-and-chicken place down the street. She didn't look at him.

There were some people standing near the elevator in the lobby, yelling and laughing loudly, and at least seven people lined up at the wall phone. Mrs. Larkin would have a wait if she decided to leave Jacob alone and call the police. But, Clay thought, she probably wouldn't.

He walked straight out the door. When he was well away from the hotel, he jammed his hands in his pockets. It was a lot colder than he'd expected.

2 Outside

Clay shivered and looked straight up. Suspended above the buildings in which people lived and worked was a luminous yellow glow as if the city was a banked fire. Above that was the huge black sky that covered everything. The neon signs of closed stores cast out fishing lines of light onto the shadowed street. In restaurants, he glimpsed a few late diners, most of them alone at their tables. In little grocery stores that stayed open all night, he saw people clutching plastic bags of fruit or cartons of milk, silently handing money to clerks.

He kept close to the buildings, watching out for a policeman who might stop to ask him what he was doing out alone so late. A clock in the window of a jewellery store showed the hour: 11:50. People walked swiftly, as though they were hastening home before something happened. Across the street, he glimpsed a group of tall boys in baseball caps and billowing nylon jackets. They weren't hurrying. They were shouting words, always the same four or five, as if they knew no other language to hurl in insult at the sky, at cars, at windows behind which, at those sounds, sleepers would be yanked from sleep just as Clay had been in the middle of the night in the hotel. That was when raging voices penetrated the walls with those same words that said, This is what human beings do on toilets and together in their beds. It was a great howling that kept Clay and his mother awake until it mumbled away into silence. He went quickly to the corner and turned to the left.

A car alarm shrieked somewhere ahead of him. His father had once remarked that car alarms told car thieves which were the best cars to steal. His mother had laughed. He pictured his mother laughing—her head would go back, her eyes would squeeze tight. Her laugh had been merry and slightly hoarse.

"Where you going?" demanded a voice.

An old man with a blue cloth tied around his head was looking down at him, one of his hands gripping a small shopping cart full of sacks.

"To get aspirin for my mother," Clay said.

"Yeah. They're not going to sell you no aspirin. They're not going to sell you nothing. Get on home."

Clay ran to the end of the block and turned another corner to find himself on a broad avenue. At that moment, the lights on the marquee of a movie theatre went out. A public telephone booth stood near the entrance. He felt the quarters in his pocket. Who could he call? He stood near the booth and watched as a man drew an iron gate in front of the lobby of the theatre and locked it. The man suddenly coughed violently, took a large handkerchief from his inside jacket pocket, and covered his face with it as he walked away. Could he see through the handkerchief? Clay wondered. He looked at the telephone.

His father's mother lived in Salem, Oregon. His father had told Clay about her. She hadn't spoken to Lawrence Garrity since he'd told her he was marrying Angela Vecchia. "Italian," she'd said. "You've ended our family line, pure English until this! I'll have nothing more to say to you. And if you have children, I'll have even less to say to them."

What was less than nothing? His mother's parents were dead. There were some cousins in Florida, but he didn't know whether they were his mother's or his father's. The Garritys were a very small family, just three people.

He went on until he came to a house that stood between two tall buildings. It had a little stoop, and he went up the stairs and sat down on the marble threshold inside the doorway. He imagined calling his grandmother in Oregon and saying, "I'm half Italian. Would you tell the other half what to do?" He almost smiled.

It was so late; yet the longest part of the night was still ahead. He wasn't too cold, but he knew he would be later on. He closed his eyes and leaned back against the portal.

He didn't know how long he'd slept. But he knew

what had waked him, thumps from inside the house. It had grown colder, and he shivered constantly as he bent his head towards the door. Someone was descending stairs. He got to his feet, took two steps at a time, and hit the sidewalk running. He didn't look back to see who it was who had come out.

He walked on. The part of the city he had come to was much darker than the area where the hotel was. He saw what he thought were warehouses. There were empty buildings, old tenements with their windows boarded up and a few narrow old houses, their stoops collapsed in heaps in front of them, their windows filled in with cement blocks. A dog emerged from an alley, whined as it looked at him, then backed away and fled down the street. Perhaps it was his imaginary dog.

He came to an opening in a long railing. There were steps leading down to an alley that was lined with dented garbage cans. He stayed there a few minutes, perhaps longer, gripping the railing as he half dozed. A cat's mewling might have been part of a dream. An ambulance siren snapped him fully awake. He rubbed his eyes as it tore by, its lights flashing, its siren wailing like a crazy person in a well.

Clay wandered on, crossing streets, turning corners, his legs aching. When he asked himself where he was going, he shut his eyes very hard for a moment, and then walked faster.

At some point, he had to pee. He found an alley

where the air smelled dead and close like very old garbage. Standing there, hidden from the street, trying to breathe shallowly, he had what was almost a vision, or a kind of mist of memory, of being lifted up by his father in the dark warmth of a room, of being carried to the bathroom, where a tiny night-light in a floor socket gave off an amber glow, and his father murmuring, "That's good, my sweetheart. You can sleep right through now."

He felt his jaw clamping and he shook his head. He mustn't remember anything for a while.

In the few cars that sped past, he could see huddled indistinct figures. At the end of a long block, a tall man stood beneath a streetlight, gesturing and shouting to himself.

Then he saw directly ahead a small triangular park like an island in a stream. There were trees, a few with mustard-coloured leaves that looked dead in the light of a street lamp. Hedges grew along an iron railing on the farther side. It was a shadowed place with patches of blackness. Leaves covered most of the paths, and an overflowing trash basket stood at the entrance.

He crossed a street and waited a moment as he heard a very faint murmur—there, and not there—whispers fading into nothing. Now he could see that the black patches were cardboard boxes and heaps of bundles and that there were many long pieces of cardboard lying about on the ground and beneath benches.

There were people in the park. On a nearby bench,

an old woman lay doubled over, apparently asleep, black plastic bags gathered around her on the bench and on the ground, like big black stones. On another bench across from her, a young man was lying, his head half off the edge, one bare foot sticking out, a shoe on the ground just beneath it. Deeper into the park, he now made out other bodies, some upright, some lying down. This could be a place where he might sleep too. He could drag a piece of cardboard under a hedge.

He found a long piece, but the branches of the hedge were too close to the ground and too scratchy for him to burrow under. A few feet away stood a van he hadn't noticed until then. He could see it was the kind that had a side opening, although it was closed down. The van was parked between two paths, on a patch of dead grass. The odd thing about it was that the tyres had been removed, and it stood on thin wheel rims.

Clay heard a voice so low it was close to a whisper.

"Look at that, Calvin," it said.

"I'm trying to get some shut-eye, Buddy," someone protested.

"A kid, wearing a nice jacket. Looking scared," Buddy said.

Clay felt his hands curl into fists.

He heard a long, drawn-out groan. By squinting hard, he could see an old man pulling scraps of blanket and a piece of canvas over his head, which poked out

from what looked like the sort of wooden crate a new
refrigerator came in.

"I'm going to get him," said Buddy.

"Let him be. It'll be on your head. He has his own
fate," said the old man.

"Yeah. Well, maybe I'm his fate."

3 Calvin and Buddy

Were they talking about him? Clay wondered. But his tiredness was so great, it didn't seem to matter. It didn't seem to leave room for fear.

He thought there was enough space beneath the van for him to crawl into. He wouldn't need the cardboard. It was almost warm there, or perhaps it was close and tight enough to be a pretend warmth.

He heard the voices going on, becoming fainter. Then, at the very edge of sleep, a man's face appeared a foot from his own. At once, the man put a finger against his lips and held it there for a long moment. Then he took the hand away and extended it towards Clay, smiling as he did so. The man's head brushed the guts of the van.

Clay covered his face. The man patted his arm gently.

"Come on," he said. "We've got a place with a roof."

After a minute, Clay wriggled out, and they both stood up. "Don't make noise," the man whispered as he led him to the wooden crate, turning at every step to make sure Clay was with him.

"You get inside with old Calvin," he told him. "You're small enough to fit." Carefully, the man pushed Calvin onto his side.

"Murder," mumbled the old man.

Clay felt he was falling asleep on his feet. "It's all right," the man said. "We'll figure it out in the morning."

Clay hesitated a moment, then crawled into the crate. The man, wrapped in a tweed coat, stood there watching him until his feet were inside along with the rest of him.

Not more than a minute later, Buddy could hear his breathing, quick and shallow. Runaway, he said to himself. Got mad about something.

He sighed and leaned back against the crate. He and Calvin took turns sleeping inside it. The tweed coat, which he'd found in a box someone had left at the park entrance, was enormous, and he was glad of it. He could nearly wrap it twice around himself.

Buddy listened. He heard a faint sound of traffic and, closer, the night noises of sleeping human beings. There were around eight tonight, he guessed, two of them regulars. The new ones must have been drawn to the park by news of the coffee van.

He thought he heard a noise, and glanced over at the hedges. He stared at the small, dull green leaves that were the last to fall, long after the trees lost theirs.

He didn't want to think about last leaves, snow and sleet and ice, and the terrible wind that come roaring up from the Hudson River and right through your skin to your bones. On really cold mornings, Buddy couldn't move his fingers when he first woke up. A nurse in the clinic, where he had gone after he'd hurt his back lugging Calvin from an alley, told him he'd have serious arthritis problems, young as he was, if he didn't get in out of the weather. He ought to go to a shelter, she'd told him—there were shelters all over the city—why didn't he go to one? Better to get arthritis, he'd told her, than get his head bashed in and his shoes stolen. "Oh, now, now!" she'd protested. "It can't be that bad!"

The boy muttered something, and stirred.

Buddy knew it was hard to sleep, especially for the new people, the ones who hadn't been on the street before. They were in a panic for days. They were also the angriest if someone or something woke them up in the middle of the night.

He looked at old Mrs. Crary nearly bent double, one thin hand gripping a sack even in her sleep, a strand of white hair lying across her cheek like a deep scar. Dimp Laughlin, who begged over on the East Side, and his mongrel dog were curled up together under newspapers that rustled very faintly as though a ghost was reading them. The dog never barked—must have lost his bark from discouragement. Buddy didn't feel easy at night walking around. People made crazy drugs, or by their lives, or just plain crazy, would jump you for looking at them. Nearby, lying on several thicknesses of cardboard, right out in the open on the path near the van, was a young man. He was wearing a thin baseball jacket, and several earrings glinted in his right ear. He was moaning softly in his sleep.

So far, Buddy and Calvin had been lucky in the park, just a doper now and then. But they would come eventually, like rats and tides and bad weather, and then Buddy and Calvin would have to find another place to live. Calvin said there were different neighbourhoods among homeless people. He said that even in hell there must be different neighbourhoods.

Gerald, the coffee and doughnut man, had light blue eyes and curly brown hair. As usual, he was wearing his thick brown sweater and a pale blue wool scarf wrapped around his neck as he moved quickly, half-stooped, behind the narrow counter of the van. He placed doughnuts on paper plates and lined up Styrofoam cups for coffee. Next to several cartons of milk was a box of cheese sandwiches Gerald and his cook had prepared before daylight.

It was 6:00 A.M. Everyone Gerald could see was awake, and from benches and beside hedges, they all looked at him in silence. Each morning there were a few new faces, but some faces from the day before would be missing. Gradually, people rose and stretched. Mrs. Crary rubbed her arms and knees and stood up. They all began to make their way to the van.

Gerald smiled and said good morning to each person in his low, even voice as he handed them out their breakfasts. He knew their sleep did not banish their tiredness. Sleep was something they had to give in to wherever they were, simply because it grew dark and their bones couldn't carry them any longer. Gerald didn't know what it was like to be homeless— he had two houses, one in the city and one in the country. But he could imagine. At home in his desk, he had a pile of summonses from the police department, warning him to remove his van from what was city property or else it would be towed away. Yesterday, Gerald had removed all the van tyres while Mrs. Crary directed him imperiously, holding a stick in the air like a baton. "And now the right rear tyre shall be removed," she had chanted.

In the wooden crate, Calvin lay awake, staring at the sleeping boy whose face he could not yet see. Gradually, he slid himself outside. Buddy had gone off to the construction site down the street where several days ago, he had successfully prised open the door of a mobile toilet for the workers. No one had bothered to fix it yet.

Calvin reached out a finger and touched the boy's leg lightly. He was real. Now he recalled Buddy's saying last night, "A kid. Wearing a nice jacket . . ."

The boy lifted his head, his eyes wide open. He saw

39

an old man with a thick, tangled white beard, muddy, sunken eyes, and hanks of grey hair hanging on either side of his long, shrunken cheeks. The boy drew a deep breath and coughed.

"The air in there leaves something to be desired," said Calvin. "The trick is to crawl outside as fast as you can."

Clay squirmed his way into the grey morning light, and the cold air that smelled of old newspapers and pavement. He sat down in front of the old man, his legs stretched out.

"Buddy has found a bathroom so as not to add to the ordure collecting around the bushes," the old man said.

Clay had not heard that word before, but he guessed what it meant.

"You can try the drinking fountain. Sometimes there's a trickle of water to wash your face with. While you're doing that, I'll go see Gerald over there in the van and see what I can get you in the way of food. What's your name?"

"Clay," said the boy.

The old man sighed. "Surely you have a last name," he said. "Only slaves and women had no last names, and that was long ago."

"Clay Garrity."

"I am Calvin Bosker," said the old man. "And Buddy is Buddy Meadowsweet. After we eat, we'll have to look into your situation."

In front of the crate, Clay sat close to Buddy, a few feet away from Calvin.

"Good?" asked Buddy of Clay. "Why don't you finish it?"

Except to name himself, Clay had not spoken. He cleared his throat. "I've never had coffee before," he said.

"It was mostly milk," Buddy said.

"Where shall I throw the cup?" Clay asked.

"Don't throw it away," replied Buddy. "Someone can use it. Like Dimp Laughlin and his dog, who beg uptown over on the east."

"We'll have rain," remarked Calvin, combing his beard with his fingers.

"You can't tell yet," Buddy said. "All mornings start grey."

"I can tell by my old bones," Calvin said crossly.

Clay was finishing his doughnut with difficulty. His throat felt as though a lump of bread had lodged in it. A light breeze swept through the park like a wispy broom, rustling leaves and newspapers. He saw people scratching, stretching, blowing their noses into rags. Some trailed back to the van, where Gerald's bright hair and bright smile shone like small beacons in the gloomy light. Clay noticed an old woman counting her bags over and over again. He could see there were six. Why did she keep counting?

Calvin appeared to have sensed his puzzlement. "Even if you don't have a roof over your head, you count your things," he said. "It's a kind of house-keeping. Most people who come here have one or two things to count—the junk people throw away so they can buy more junk. Where do they think *away* is?"

"We're away," Buddy said.

Calvin looked hard at Clay. "How old are you?" he asked sternly.

Clay ducked his head.

"I might guess," Calvin said.

"Eleven," Clay answered.

"It's storytelling time," Buddy said in a kindly way, smiling at Clay. "We'll tell you about us. But first you got to tell us about you."

Suddenly Clay was afraid. By now, Mrs. Larkin had probably taken Jacob to the lobby in the hotel, holding on to him while she called the police. They might be looking for him. And if Mrs. Larkin hadn't called the police, Buddy and Calvin would. He had to get back to the room, to see if Ma had returned. He felt his legs tense for running.

"Did you leave home for some stupid reason?" Calvin asked.

"He's too little for something like that," Buddy said. "You got to be grown-up to be really stupid."

"Speak up, Clay. Buddy and I aren't going to do anything but listen. And the cars will be along soon to deafen us, honking and thumping and squealing. Go on, now."

The man with the dog was walking out of the park.

Clay saw him hold out a slice of cheese. The dog took it gently in its jaws.

"Are you going to call the police about me?" Clay asked.

He saw a glance pass between Buddy and Calvin, but he couldn't read it. Buddy said, "I don't call the police. Calvin doesn't call the police. You're big enough to call them yourself . . . if that's what's right to do."

Clay plunged in. "My father lost his job," he began. "The magazine where he worked folded. After a while, he went away. My mother worked in an office at night. She's going to have a baby. We went to a lot of offices like Social Services, where you wait all day and they give you papers to fill out. Then we couldn't pay the rent. Daddy didn't write or anything like that. We had to move to a hotel, and I had to go to a different school. Then Ma went away, six days ago. There's a woman in the hotel who's probably called the police by now to tell them about Ma and me. But Ma might have come back. She might be there right now."

Calvin and Buddy looked at him silently for a moment. A black squirrel ran straight up the trunk of a nearby tree.

"That's a big story for one so young," remarked Calvin.

"My story is short," Buddy said. "I left home in Columbia, South Carolina, with sixty-eight dollars and a stamp to put on a letter home when I got here. I was seventeen, but I could pass for twenty. First, I worked in a zoo, cleaning, feeding the animals . . . like that. But they had to cut back. What they cut back was me. I worked as a janitor, had a little room of my own. After a year, the building started selling apartments instead of renting them, and the maintenance people, me again, got fired. I could have got more jobs, but I didn't have money for a place to live. I went all over the place, looking, and twice I stayed in shelters. First thing they took was my good shoes. So I moved to the sidewalk. I met Calvin a few months ago, and here we are." Buddy paused a moment and shook his head. "I never did get to use that stamp. I was waiting for good news to tell them at home. What I do now is collect the cans people throw away and I get a nickel for each one. So I've always got a dollar or two."

"Yes, he met me," Calvin went on. "He saved my life . . . I don't know what for. I have a son who lives in Hawaii. I doubt we'd recognise each other. It's been a quarter of a century since we last spoke. I used to teach mathematics to tenth-grade students who didn't want to know the time of day. I did that for years, and when I retired, I was happy. I had a little apartment above a restaurant in Brooklyn, and the best record collection I ever came across. Oh, my music . . . gone now. Early one winter morning, a fire started in the restaurant. My apartment burned up, and all my records and tapes. I had no savings. I lived in hotels, then a rooming house. The woman who owned it went off to California. My pension cheques followed me for a while. Then I found the street. It had been there all the time—I simply hadn't realised it. Sometimes I drink too much liquor. Buddy found me in an alley halfway under a laundry truck. Buddy has a reasonable mind—he figured that when the driver went to work that morning, he might not see me, and when he started up his truck, bang! There would have gone Calvin Bosker. My story is really over."

"Don't talk that way," Buddy said. "It isn't over. And mine isn't nor Clay's."

"Clay. Are you a lost child?" Calvin asked with sudden ferocity.

Clay knew there were thousands of lost children. Some had run away from their homes; some had been taken. His mother warned him often not to talk to anyone he didn't know. But that was then.

"I'm not really lost," he said to Calvin. "It's just that I've got to go back to the hotel—see if Ma is there."

"Ma . . ." echoed Buddy.

Down the street on the other side of the park, past a huge warehouselike building that looked empty of life, came a jogger. His face was as expressionless as a white plate. He wore earphones. As he passed the park, they could hear his breathing and the thump of his running shoes on the pavement.

"He would do better to strengthen the muscles of

his brain," remarked Calvin. He turned to Clay. "Now we must do our housework. Before you go to the hotel, please gather up some newspapers. We need them for the cold. I'm going to air out our abode."

"I'm going to work," said Buddy.

As Clay went about collecting the yellowed sheets of newspaper, he saw the old lady eating a cheese sandwich very slowly, taking little bites and holding up her head to the sky between each one, like a bird drinking water. All the other people who had slept in the park that night had disappeared.

"I hope your mother will be there," Calvin said to him when he returned with an armful of newspapers. "But if she isn't, you must come back to us. Don't wander around the streets. There are nightmares walking around looking somewhat human. But they aren't."

As Clay passed the van, Gerald looked up. "I have an extra doughnut," he said. "You can share it with your mother."

Clay didn't tell him he was alone, that his mother wasn't there, that he didn't know where on earth she was, that his heart was beating with dread and hope. He took the doughnut and said thank you and was rewarded by Gerald's sunny smile.

4 Escaping Notice

The hotel was closer to the park than Clay had imagined. His journey last night had seemed so long, and he was surprised, after twenty-five minutes and two wrong turns, to emerge on the familiar street. As he looked down its length, he felt fear like a feather drawn lightly downward from his brow to his belly, as though he saw for the first time the place where he and his mother had come to live.

It was such a squat, ugly building, its window ledges crowded with jars and bottles and milk cartons, the dirty windows seeming to darken before his eyes as the early morning light strengthened. The lobby doors were wide open as if there was nothing inside to be kept safe and private.

Two women joggers wearing purple shorts moved like jumping jacks along the line of parked cars. They didn't notice Clay. They didn't appear to notice anything. That morning people hadn't yet begun to come out of the apartment building to go to work. A few cars sped along the street as though there were no more traffic lights in the city.

A few feet from the hotel entrance, Tony, a boy Clay had spoken to now and then in the corridors or the lobby, was curled up against the brick wall, asleep. Clay peered through the doors. No one was inside. Cigarette butts covered the stained brown carpet. When you walked on it, it gave off a swampy smell like damp cigarettes. In the hard grey dirt alongside the building where hedges might once have grown, he saw five used hypodermic needles. If he looked further, he knew he would find more.

The door to the stairs would probably be locked at this hour. He'd have to take the elevator—the poison box—to the fifth floor.

"Good morning," said a thin, soft voice. He turned from the entrance. Tony was sitting on the sidewalk, gripping his knees with his arms, looking up at Clay.

Tony spoke like a grown-up; he had a kind of formality that he kept even when other children made fun of him or cursed him. He would regard them silently, a slight smile on his face, as if they were puzzling but not very interesting aliens from another planet.

"Good morning," Clay replied.

"You've been out?" asked Tony.

Clay nodded.

"I've been out, too, all night," said Tony.

There was a red bruise on his right cheek. It looked warm like a dying coal.

"I better get upstairs," he said. "You going in?"

"We'll have to take the elevator," Clay said. Tony shrugged as though that wouldn't matter.

Tony was thin as a stick. He wore a belt that went twice around his waist. Clay guessed it was his father's. All except the top button was missing from his green cotton shirt that looked like a girl's.

The only sound in the lobby was the elevator descending, until a car revved up loudly out on the street. The elevator door opened and closed like a trap—*snap!* You had to move fast getting in or out. There were new messages spray painted on the walls. One small neat one, written in red crayon, said STOP.

"The daily news," Tony said, waving at the walls. Then, with no change in his voice, he said, "My father threw the television out the window last night. It didn't conk anybody, because it fell into the air shaft."

"Why did he do that?" Clay asked, embarrassed.

"He got mad because he couldn't get the volume up," Tony said. He added, "You never can tell."

Tony's father was the terror of the seventh floor. People ran into their rooms when they heard his door open. Clay had frequently seen Tony's mother in the lobby with Tony and his two small sisters, a suitcase and some shopping bags at their feet, as though they were about to leave the hotel. So far they hadn't.

Clay tried not to stare at the bruise on Tony's cheek. He knew who had given it to him.

"Goodbye," Tony said politely as Clay got off on the fifth floor.

For a moment, as he walked down the corridor, Clay thought of what Tony was going home to on the seventh floor.

But in the silent, dirty corridor, his heart began to pound loudly. He could feel it in his throat as though it had crawled up there out of fear. When he unlocked the door, his mother would be asleep in her bed, lying on her back, the bump of the new baby making a round mound like a soccer ball under the blanket. "Ma . . ." he whispered as he pushed the door open.

The room was washed grey by morning light. Everything was as he had left it, her rumpled brown coat on his cot, the soot-streaked windows, clothes pushed into a bunch on the rack. No one. Silence. Hadn't he known she wouldn't be there?

The only colour in the room was a red crayon lying on a table where they ate and where his mother filled in forms for Social Services.

The red crayon was one he used to make his own mark on the elevator walls, the corridor walls, sometimes on a patch of sidewalk. The word he always wrote was STOP. He didn't think people would notice it, because they loved the sex and bathroom words so much, although he had noticed when he rode up in the elevator with Tony that his mark stood out. He didn't know what he meant by it, but when he glimpsed it as he went about his day, doing errands and going to school, it made him feel like a spy, his mark stronger than all the other words. There was something about it that amused him, too, in a secret way. He slid the crayon into his pocket.

In the book box, there was an envelope that held a few photographs. He might take one of his mother and father standing near the sailing pond in Central Park to show Calvin and Buddy. What an awful idea! A lie! Instead, he took his copy of *Robinson Crusoe*.

He ought to go. Mrs. Larkin might hear him moving around. He took some socks and underwear and a T-shirt from the suitcase and put them in a paper bag he found beneath the cooking table. A thought slid into his mind. Now *he* was running away, leaving the hotel. But he would keep a watch on it. He'd find places along the street so that if his mother came back, he'd spot her.

Ma had said his father couldn't bear it. Now she had gone. Had she, too, not been able to bear it? Was *it* him? He let himself sink into the question for a minute. He knew that wasn't so.

It was because everything had fallen away—Daddy, the apartment, things like a television set, a refrigerator, cushions and frying pans, a private bathroom, a telephone, a place of one's own, a private place among millions of people.

But his mother shouldn't have gone and left him. It was terrible that she had done that.

51

He left the room. Radios were playing now. He could hear the rise and fall of many voices. He hurried to the stairway, hoping the first-floor door would be unlocked by this time.

There was dope stuff scattered on the stairs and a few chicken bones and lots of cellophane wrappers and crushed cigarette packs. "Ordure," he said aloud, another kind than Calvin had meant. He thought of Buddy and Calvin. It didn't make him happy but he felt slightly less alone.

The first-floor door was locked. He'd have to wait until the security man unlocked it, and then he could get away.

He sat down on a step, suddenly very sleepy. If only his mother had left a note, a word, "I'll be back soon . . . ." or "I've gone to have the baby. . . ." What if something had happened to her? An accident? She'd been so blurry these last weeks, like an out-of-focus snapshot. For a long while, he'd missed her quick understanding glance that was nearly always on her face when he looked her way, that seemed to take in everything about him.

His head felt so heavy. He leaned against the railing and almost at once fell asleep.

When he woke up, he could hear the late morning noises beyond the heavy metal door. They were the sounds he heard every Saturday when he ran down the stairs to get out of the room. People spoke excitedly, sometimes in languages he didn't understand. There

52

were always grumbling arguments that trailed off suddenly into silence, and shrieks of laughter that could suddenly turn into screams.

He stood up and tried the door. It was open. He wondered if anyone had passed him while he slept. There was a trail of coffee grounds on the stairs nearby. Someone must have lugged down a leaking garbage sack. He peeked through the door.

People were lined up at the telephone. He heard someone shout, "But I *been* waiting now two months!" A huge woman sat on a bench with two babies climbing up and tumbling down from her lap, both of them tied to her by long cords that stretched from their waists to her wrists.

Nobody looked at him. He was used to that. Still, he didn't count on it. Now and then a person would catch sight of him. He'd been chased all over the hotel, down corridors and up the stairs, once to the roof, where he had hid for hours behind a chimney pot. It was that sudden shift of attention he had to keep himself ready for. Watch out. Stay on your toes, his mother had said.

He slipped out through the lobby to the sidewalk.

He wouldn't be able to watch for his mother from under the awning of the apartment house across the street. If a kid from the hotel went near the entrance, the doorman, usually leaning up against the wall inside, would start up like a battery-run machine, his feet hitting the floor with great thumps, his elbows pumping, his mouth opening to shout, "Bums! Bums, get going!"

There were sparse hedges he could get behind, an entrance to a dentist's office, other entries to small stores, and the subway exit at the corner. He could take shelter there if a policeman came along.

There was another place, the news store, diagonally across the street from the hotel, where Abdul, the Arab owner, appeared to dream behind a counter covered with packs of cigarettes, candy, and little packages of cheese and peanut butter crackers. Abdul never seemed to mind his looking at magazine covers as long as he didn't pick them up. And from inside the store, he could see people as they went by.

But Abdul knew about school hours, though he looked as if he minded no one's business but his own as he made change, putting magazines in a thin paper bag if a customer asked for one, his eyes looking off somewhere into the distance. Clay knew Abdul recognised him by now, and even might ask him a dangerous question about school in his deep voice. Still, it was Saturday, and he would run in there if he saw a policeman.

For a long time, Clay stood near the subway exit until he felt so hungry he didn't even dare look towards Abdul's. He'd seen Tony pinch candy, doing it swiftly, loading up the pockets of his oversize pants. One day Abdul caught him at it, and now Tony wasn't allowed in the store.

Suddenly, Clay recollected the money he'd taken from beneath the doughnut box in the hotel room and that was now in his pocket. He went into the news store and bought two packages of cheese and peanut butter crackers, a soda, and a coconut bar. Abdul took the money Clay handed him and gave him change, silent and unquestioning as usual.

Clay walked along the sidewalk, eating. His father would not have liked that. "Animals eat on the run," he had said once. But that was before, when the Garritys had a small, pleasant kitchen, and a table to eat on, and the outside world of streets and sidewalks was something you passed through to get to other inside places. Even his father might be eating on a street somewhere at this moment. When he finished the soda, he started to throw the can into a trash basket. Then he remembered Buddy's job and held on to it.

He must have been hanging around the hotel for hours by now. His legs ached. His fingers had stiffened around the can which was too big to fit into a pocket. What he had to do was to sit down, and the only place where he could do that without people noticing him was the little park. He could come back later to keep watch, perhaps after dark.

Calvin was sitting at the entrance to the crate, his legs stretched in front of him, a notebook on his lap. It was the same kind that Clay used in school, except that

Calvin's notebook looked like it was about to fall apart. He was writing in it fiercely, pressing the stub of a pencil hard against a page. On the ground beside him were two small wrinkled apples.

Clay stood silently a moment. He felt timid in front of the old man with his long beard and his strange, cold glance. Buddy was so different, almost neat even when he had worn the raggedy coat over his blue jeans and T-shirt. His crinkly curls grew tight on his head like a black cap, his skin was smooth and dark brown, and he was quick to smile.

Calvin looked up. "You want one of my apples?" he asked. "They fell off a fruit cart. . . . They're a bit old, but sweet, I'd guess." He held one out to Clay, who took it and ate it, more out of gratitude that Calvin had given him something than from hunger. He felt a little sick. The candy bar had been a mistake.

"Was she there?" Calvin asked as if he already knew the answer, which he went on to show he did. "Well, of course not. Or else you wouldn't be here."

Clay said nothing.

"I haven't thought much about these matters," Calvin continued. "I do not think about children any more if I can help it. But I am sure you ought to take yourself off to the local police station. Someone may be looking for you. Don't look so frightened. You're not a criminal."

"There are agencies," Clay said hurriedly. "They would take me away to someplace for good. I won't be able to look for my mother any more." His voice had risen, though he had meant to try and speak calmly. He moved further away from Calvin. "What if she comes back and I'm gone?"

"Then she would go to such an agency and find you," Calvin said. He spoke evenly, not looking at Clay. "Foster homes. They can be good and bad. At least you'd have a bed of your own and three meals a day, and you'd go to school."

He looked up at Clay. "You must go to school," he said. "If you don't learn a few things in this world, you'll be as empty as that can you're carrying." Clay dropped the can on the ground. "Besides," Calvin added, "the world will be a dull, dead place if you stay ignorant."

Clay's attention was distracted by a movement he glimpsed on the sidewalk. A skinny dog was loping along, cringing as it looked up at the people walking around it. Clay felt awful about lost animals, the kittens set loose in the hotel corridors to starve, the dogs picked up by kids from the street, only to be abandoned or beaten. They were like babies, all the lost animals, babies who couldn't tell you how they were suffering.

Clay squatted down, facing Calvin. "If I go to a foster home," he said, "I'll never see my mother and father again. We'll be lost from each other forever."

"You don't know that," the old man retorted. "None of us knows what's ahead."

"Folks!" cried Buddy as he hurried towards them down the path.

"It's *folk*," said Calvin dryly. "A collective noun like *sheep* or *fish*."

"Okay. Folk," Buddy said, laughing. "Listen to what happened to me. I was looking for my cans and I found this little shopping bag at the bottom of a trash basket. Inside it was a bunch of credit cards, a driver's licence, and stuff like that. So I went to a phone and got the number from information for the name on the licence. And a man answered, and I told him what I'd found. And he said his wife's purse had been snatched this morning on the subway. He couldn't thank me enough, he said. We made an arrangement, and he drove down from the Bronx over to the corner of White Street, where I was waiting. He was this elderly fellow and he looked me over and I gave him the bag and he gave me thirty-five dollars. Folk! We're going to eat tonight! I'm taking you to the diner over on Ninth Avenue. I tell you there are saints in this world!"

"There are no saints," Calvin said ferociously.

"There's Gerald," Buddy said. "And the ones who bring the boxes of clothing. And the ones at the church. And that old fellow giving me that money for those cards he won't be able to use anyhow. Come on, Calvin!"

Calvin said, "All right, all right . . . maybe there are three saints. Not more, I think."

5 The Coffee Van

"What are you writing, Calvin?" Clay asked.

"A history of my life and times," Calvin replied, glancing over at Clay, who had let *Robinson Crusoe* fall onto his lap.

It was early morning, a quiet time before the heavier traffic started up. Gerald had been bringing extra milk for Clay, who had begun to like it with a drop of coffee for warmth. He finished it now and put the cup inside the crate for Dimp Laughlin and his dog, even though Dimp hadn't been around for a few days. Yesterday, the cold had been bitter, the sky the colour of metal. But today, though it was dank, there were rays of pale, mothy sunlight that Clay watched move across the scattered newspapers people had slept beneath, discarded garbage sacks, a mud-caked boot on its side under a bench, the grainy surface of the drinking fountain that no longer worked.

In the two weeks Clay had been living in the park, Buddy had found several things to improve their living arrangement—a crescent of hard plastic that now shielded the entrance of the crate, another piece of tarp to cover its west side, which took the brunt of the river wind, and a straight-backed chair in which Calvin was at present sitting, his feet in slippers that appeared to have been cut out of an old pink carpet.

There were a few people clustered at the counter of the van. Buddy had left on his daily round to find cans to redeem, saying it would be a good morning because of all he'd eaten at the Unitarian Church several blocks away, where he and Clay and Calvin had gone for Thanksgiving dinner. Wrapped tightly in plastic and hidden in the back of the crate was a paper dish full of left-over turkey parts, hard to chew but still pretty good.

"Is your life going to fit inside that notebook?" Clay asked.

"This is the eleventh notebook I've filled," Calvin replied. "I'm up to age forty-seven."

"You told me the story of your life when I first came, and it took you about three minutes," Clay remarked.

"That was an outline. Each time you tell the story, there's more. . . . Any life is infinite. Imagine a single hour, all that happens in it."

"But what if I'm reading, or just staring at something for an hour?" asked Clay.

"Do you think your brain leaves town? It's always working, with or without your permission. What you think and feel is as much of a story as the things that happen outside you."

Clay didn't entirely understand what the old man was saying, but he was grateful to have a conversation with him, especially since Calvin wasn't, as he often was, talking about Clay going to the police and foster homes.

Sometimes the two men paid little attention to him, although he knew they had really taken him into their lives in the park.

But on some days, there had been moments, hours, when they barely spoke to him as they went about their housekeeping, or just sat silently with grim, faraway expressions on their faces. Then he knew that his being a child, a thing he'd never thought about much before, made no difference at all. He was alone as they were alone. He was just another person, ageless, in trouble, out of ordinary life, out of the time that ruled the lives of people hurrying past the park on their way to work or home.

"Do you know something, Clay?" Calvin's voice broke into his thoughts. "You need a haircut."

He was a fine one to talk, Clay thought to himself. Birds could have built nests in his hair and beard.

"It's different for me," said Calvin. "I'm an old tree. But you look merely ratty. Now, don't sulk."

"I'm not," Clay protested.

"Your face is sulking. Do something about it. Just let me trim your hair. I have a pair of scissors somewhere, dull, but they'll do."

"But—what for?" asked Clay.

"To hold on to neatness, call it staying neat in a cyclone. Call it what you like. All of us, living as we must, disgust the people who bother to look at us. They blame us for the way we look and smell. They're scared of really poor people."

"But poor people are scared of each other too," Clay said, thinking about the hotel.

"That's true, but the reasons are different. As I was saying, people begin to think of us as nasty stains on the sidewalk, nasty things in their way." He paused and looked up at the sky. "I think we'll have snow one of these days soon." He went to the crate, leaned inside, and began to rummage in one of his sacks, from which he soon drew a small pair of scissors.

He came back to the chair, saying, "When I was young, you could make up a life . . . a little work here or there . . . keep yourself decent . . . even save a few dollars. If Robinson Crusoe was washed up on the shores of that island nowadays, he'd find a used car lot there, and before he could get a job sweeping the asphalt, he'd be asked for his papers, his degrees, and his work background."

Clay sat down on the ground in front of Calvin. It was just as the old man had finished trimming the hair on his neck that Clay looked up and saw a patrol car, a flatbed truck, and a police emergency van draw up to the park entrance.

Gerald, wearing a sweater with a turtleneck that nearly covered his chin, was handing out the last cheese sandwich to a young woman with a head of wild, frizzy hair dyed purple. An enormous shawl covered her except for the pale hand that reached for the sandwich. Calvin's hand holding the scissors fell lightly on Clay's shoulder. Ten policemen and several men in work clothes walked determinedly towards the van. Gerald ran out from behind the counter to the rear and spread his arms wide. "No! Please!" he shouted.

"What's going to happen?" Clay asked urgently.

"Hush!" commanded Calvin.

Mrs. Crary, with a speed Clay would not have thought her capable of, gathered up her bundles and scuttled out into the street, followed by the young woman in the shawl, still chewing on her sandwich.

Ignoring Gerald, all the men lined up around the van, bent, and lifted it. Clay could hear them grunting with effort as they carried it out to the street, right past Gerald, where it was loaded onto the flatbed.

Gerald remained standing in the bare place where the van had stood on its rims. A policeman came up to him and handed him some papers and walked away.

The work crew and the police got into their vehicles. There was a clanging of gears, a revving of motors. Then they were gone. Gerald, looking dazed, made his way over to Calvin and Clay.

For a long moment, he and Calvin stared at each other.

"Why?" he uttered at last.

"The park is public property," replied Calvin.

Gerald shook his head. "Why?" he repeated more softly. "Why aren't they ashamed? Why did they look like stones? Why isn't everyone ashamed?"

"They don't want to study shame," Calvin said almost gently.

"Is this boy your grandson?" Gerald asked.

"Yes," said Calvin at once.

"I'm coming back tomorrow. I'll carry the food with me. They can't stop me handing coffee and sandwiches out of a taxi, can they?"

"Not as long as you pay for it," said Calvin.

Gerald hunched his shoulders and walked away from them out to the street.

"I said that—about your being my grandson—because Gerald would feel he had to do something about you. And I'm coming around to the view that Buddy and I ought to do it. The cold is coming, the real cold. There's a point you don't know about, a point where you won't want to go to school any more, won't want any of the things you miss now. You will have learned the street and you won't want to give it up."

"I can't yet," Clay said, nearly crying. "She might still come back."

"A few more days, then," Calvin said sternly. "But you're not spending Christmas in this place. Nobody ever heard of it here."

That day, when Clay returned to the hotel, there were more policemen, four of them carrying an elderly black man out of the lobby to the street. He was clutching an old down jacket to his chest like a shield.

"Now, Morgan," said one of the policeman in a placating tone of voice. "You know you've been feeling bad, setting fire to your bed like that. We are here just to help you—"

"My name is Mr. Johnson, Morgan Johnson," the black man shouted as he tried to twist away from restraining arms.

"Mr. Johnson," said another policeman. "We have to take you to the hospital."

"Call it the bin, you damned toy men!" Mr. Johnson cried as tears ran down his face.

Clay, pressing himself against the wall near the door that led to the stairs, saw them lift the old man into an ambulance that waited behind patrol cars, its lights flashing and circling. He went through the fire door and up the stairs. A thin girl, her head down, wearing a man's suit jacket over a dirty white skirt, passed him. "You gotta match? I gotta cigarette," she muttered.

In the corridor, he stood for a moment by the exit door from the stairs. There was no plastic bag outside Mrs. Larkin's door. He could see it was ajar. She always locked the door. He tiptoed to it and listened. Nothing. He pushed it open. The room was empty except for the small stove.

They had gone. Where?

He walked into the room and looked at the place where the bed had been, where he had seen Jacob fall sideways and Mrs. Larkin had set him upright and patted his hair. There was a loud thump on the wall that separated him from his old room. A baby cried. A woman's voice called out, "I'm getting it ready—now simmer down, you kids!"

He leaned against the wall. People had moved in. His mother hadn't come back. He stayed there in the empty room for a long time. At last, he took his red crayon from his pocket and wrote STOP on the wall above the corner of the little stove. But nothing stopped as he felt the whole earth growing larger and larger with himself standing in the middle of it, motionless. He dropped the crayon on the floor.

Clay wandered the streets in the afternoon, no longer fearing he would attract the notice of a policeman. He'd seen an army of them that day. They hadn't given him a glance. How could he have ever imagined they were after him? Nobody was after him.

The days were so short. Night began early. A wind was blowing the cold air right to his bones. His corduroy jacket was dirty and ragged now. He put the collar up, but it didn't do much good. His head itched from the lice Calvin had explained to him people got from living outside, like the sores on his feet and ankles and wrists. "The lice need a home too," Calvin had said in his sarcastic voice. And he had smiled sourly. "Little fellows looking for their place in the sun."

Clay imagined that instead of returning to the park, he would walk to where the city ended. There would be country, and fields, a farm where someone would take him in and give him warm chocolate milk and a bath. That was what Calvin called "making a movie in your head".

He was a truant. His mother was a runaway, and his father had disappeared. His own face would show up on a milk carton.

When he got back to the park, Buddy was there beside the crate talking to Calvin. Usually, Buddy smiled a welcome when he saw Clay, but not this time. He only stared at him as if he didn't know him.

"It was only a matter of time," Calvin was saying, "until they took Gerald's van away. He knew it too. But he couldn't stand thinking about it."

"He was just trying to do good," Buddy said.

"He can afford it," Calvin said curtly.

"They don't care if we all die out here," Buddy said. All at once, he seemed to see Clay, and he touched his shoulder. Clay stepped closer to him.

"Now, Buddy, you know we don't die in this country. We just become celestial hamburgers."

Buddy snorted with laughter. "May I be covered with piccalilli," he said.

Clay spoke. "Somebody's moved into our room. They must know my mother's not coming back."

The two men looked at him. They didn't seem surprised.

"I brought you something," Buddy said. "Got it from the Loving Heart Recycled Clothes Centre."

He reached into the crate and pulled out a dark blue wool sweater.

"I know it's too big, but it'll keep you warm for a time," he said.

Clay put it on. The sleeves covered his hands. Buddy stooped and rolled up each one to Clay's wrists. Then he did what Clay wanted him to do. He put his arms around him and held him. Clay's face was against Buddy's neck, against the warm brown flesh, feeling the steady beating of Buddy's pulse as though it was his own heartbeat.

6 Monkey Island

Calvin wore a blue watch cap pulled down over his ears and a faded pink-and-white cotton blanket wrapped around his shoulders. "Wear every bit of your clothing in case you have to skedaddle," he had advised Clay.

He was sitting in front of the crate, the inside of which was now lined with rolled newspapers. Although it was Friday, the noise of traffic was muted. A thin layer of snow, the first of the winter, covered the park, the benches and iron railing, and the streets. The twigs of trees were sheathed in ice.

Buddy was groaning softly, rubbing the backs of his ankles. Clay knew that his chilblains were hurting him. Buddy had on a pair of cotton work gloves he'd picked up somewhere. "Picked up somewhere" was how he described most of his finds.

The cold was intense. It had been three mornings since Gerald had last appeared with a big thermos of coffee, wrapped sandwiches, and doughnuts, stepping out of a taxi and calling for someone to come and help him carry the food into the park.

He was probably in court, Calvin said, defending his dastardly deed of bringing breakfast to people, and trying to get his van back.

Clay couldn't stop shivering. The coughing that had begun the day after he made his last trip to the hotel was dry and deep and made his ribs ache. He would have liked to crawl into the back of the crate and pile everything in it over himself. They'd had soda and pretzels for breakfast, which Buddy had bought with the last of Clay's money, the rest of which Clay had spent in Abdul's during the days he had kept watch on the hotel. His stomach felt queasy.

"It's time for a conference," Calvin said, a vapour cloud around his beard.

"What we need is a fire," Buddy said. "I was down by the old warehouses on the riverfront yesterday, and I saw these guys burning wood in big metal barrels. Oh, that fire looked good! If we could get a pail, you know what I mean, Calvin? I could find some coal somewhere—"

"You won't find coal. It's not used any more—"

"All right, then. Wood and a big stone or two. We could heat the stones and put them under that stuff in the crate and be warm at least part of the night."

"Yesterday evening, I was walking down White Street," Calvin said, "and I got tired and sat down in front of one of those dusty-looking fabric stores they have there. First thing you know, two cops came up and said they were taking me to a shelter. I was too old—they called me a 'geezer'—to be out in this weather. I went limp and they hauled and pulled and I went limper. They let go for a second, and I got away. I should say—I scuttled. You can usually surprise people."

"You were saying," Buddy said, "about a conference." Buddy frequently reminded Calvin of what he'd set out to talk about.

"The conference is about you, Clay," Calvin said. "Wherever your mother is, she's not going back to the hotel."

Maybe the baby had been born, Clay was thinking. It would be Lucy or Daniel. Those were the two names he'd chosen when he'd first known about the baby.

"Clay! Listen to me!"

Ma might be thinking of him this second. He felt himself shrinking to a pinpoint, to a word: *Clay*. That was what happened when he thought of her thinking of him.

"We're going to have to take you to some authority"—here Calvin paused and repeated "authority" with cold dislike—"people who'll find a home for you . . . a home with heat and regular meals and a pillow to lay your head on at night. You know that, Clay. You're dreadfully thin, you're cold all the time, you've been coughing like a chain-smoker. We can't help it that the life here is so hard. But we can help you get out of it."

71

Clay felt a sound starting in the pit of his stomach and getting bigger and bigger until it flew out of his mouth.

"No!" he cried.

"Christmas is coming," Buddy said quickly. "You could be somewhere where it'll really be Christmas."

"This doghouse is coming apart. It won't last another week," Calvin went on severely. "Listen to me. We live in days, not weeks and months. Each day can be a year. We think . . . at the end of a day . . . how we made it. Again. Only because we found an old coat, only because some people don't bother to turn in their cans and bottles, only because somebody gives me change, somebody who doesn't care if I make a few dollars that way because such a somebody knows what a terrible life it is. Other people say, You *like* the pavement—you must be making hundreds of dollars a week! Maybe some of us do, but we have to lick the sidewalks for it. Clay! I see how hard you're trying not to hear me! On Monday, Buddy is going to take you to an agency that looks out for children. You think you know all about agencies. You don't! Not everyone is like that Miss You-can't-fool-me you told us about. There are people who worry about children like you, whose hearts burn up each day of their lives and fly away at night like an ash, so they have to find a new heart every morning just to bear it all. How do you know Buddy won't find someone like that? You hear me, Clay?"

"Why can't you both take care of me?" Clay pleaded. "I could even go to school."

"Yes, and I could go with you on Father's Day," Calvin said. "I can see it now. Me, sitting at the back of the classroom with all the daddies. I look crazy and I am crazy. But—" The old man suddenly gasped as though he'd run out of breath entirely. Buddy clasped his shoulders.

"Monday, Clay," Calvin whispered. He crawled inside the crate, drawing all the tatters and rags about himself until nothing showed but a few white hairs gleaming in the shadows like silver threads.

For the first time, that day, Clay went with Buddy to his "job".

He held garbage bags open while Buddy picked through them. They walked into alleys alongside apartment houses and went through piles of rubbish. Atop walls, Clay saw huge coils of razor-edged wire that looked as if it could kill you if you stared at it long enough. He kept his eyes on the gutters, where Buddy said he sometimes found change. In all the hustling crowds whose feet were stirring the snow into slush, hardly anyone glanced at them, a young white boy and a young black man, as they went through the city looking for discarded or lost things.

After a few hours, they went to a supermarket, where Buddy redeemed the cans they had found for $3.05. They had to stand in line for nearly half an hour, along with other people who carried bags of cans. But Clay was glad for the time indoors. His feet had grown so numb he couldn't feel them.

Beneath the stoop of an old house with bricked-up windows, Buddy spotted a dented, rusty pail.

"Look at that," he said. "That's what luck is. We got a stove, Clay."

Buddy put the other things they'd found in the pail, a light bulb still in its paper case—"We might find a lamp," he said—a crochet needle, its question-mark head nearly worn away, a small leather bag with a broken strap, a paper bag filled with old socks, a small framed picture of a large dog sitting on a lawn, and some half-eaten sandwiches and pastries.

"We'll buy hot dogs and potato salad at that deli across the street," Buddy said. "We can cook the dogs over the fire. Keep your eye out for wood."

By the time they'd returned to the park, they had gathered enough scraps of wood from construction sites to make a fire in the pail. They cooked their franks on twigs Buddy broke off from a tree. Calvin brought out three spoons from what he called his kitchen bag, and they each had a small scoop of potato salad.

While they were eating, a woman with an enormous turban around her head made of stockings ambled over to them, holding out an entire apple pie.

"Warm my hands at your fire. Give you pie," she said in a gravelly voice. Clay saw that most of her teeth were missing when she suddenly smiled at him.

She squatted down and held her hands out above the pail.

Buddy cut pieces of the pie with the crochet needle. "Everything comes in handy," he whispered to Clay.

At the first taste of the apples in the sweet, half-frozen syrup, Clay felt sick. But he didn't care. He gulped down his piece. For once, his stomach was filled.

Calvin refused pie.

The woman stared at him suspiciously.

"You think I pinched this?" she cried. "It fell off a bakery wagon. That's what happened. What do they know about what falls off their damned wagons! Tell me that!"

"My digestive system is not up to it," Calvin said mildly. "Calm down. It's none of my business where you got the pie. The boy is glad, and so is Buddy."

"Don't often get a treat," Buddy said.

But the woman looked at them indignantly and grapped up the rest of the pie and walked away.

"I believe that is a person who thinks nothing is happening unless she is talking," Calvin said.

"She's crazy," Buddy said.

"Just what I said," Calvin snapped as he crawled into the crate.

The wood in the pail had burned down to ashes. Now the cold clung to Clay like a coat of chilled water. As always he had a moment of dread before he slid into the crate, a sense that he was about to be trapped inside a box from which he might not be able to escape. He looked over at Buddy, who was standing beneath the nearby tree knocking ashes out of the pail. Only an occasional car sped past the park, its roof briefly reflecting the glitter of the streetlight.

Suddenly, Buddy dropped the pail on the ground. It clanged once. He stood motionless, his head up, listening.

Clay began to hear a sound like people singing different songs at the same time. It changed into a tuneless roaring. Down the street on the opposite side of the park came what looked like a small crowd. As they passed into the light, he saw fourteen or fifteen young men and, walking by themselves a few yards behind, three girls, their arms linked, the tangle of their hair above their chalky faces like small brush fires. All of their mouths were open like people in pictures of Christmas carolers.

They were not singing carols. They were shouting, "Monkey Island! Monkey Island! Where the monkeys live!"

Calvin stuck his head out of the crate. Clay saw the turbaned woman run out of the other side of the park. Two men, barely visible beneath rags and newspapers, rose from the ground like otters and swam away into the dark.

What gleamed so dully? Clay blinked, opened his eyes wide, and stared. The men held lengths of chain and baseball bats. "Monkey Island!" they howled.

"We got to get out of here," Buddy said urgently, but he didn't move.

Calvin was crouching by the crate. "The stump people . . . out for a night's sport," he muttered.

The three girls danced in a circle in the middle of the street, their screechy laughter as piercing as shards of glass. The men had begun to hit the railing with their chains and bats. Now their chant had changed, but the words were as familiar to Clay as his own name, written on walls or shouted and grunted and hissed everywhere he had ever been in the city.

They caught sight of Buddy. "Nigger!" they cried out in one great shout, and they hit the railing with greater force while they swayed from side to side like huge red worms in a tin can.

Clay felt Calvin and Buddy grip his arms. They ran, Calvin stumbling and groaning, towards the farthest exit from the park. Down the street they went, turned, turned again, running for what seemed hours, until suddenly Buddy halted.

Calvin was panting like a thirsty dog. Clay could hardly stand upright. All he heard now above the hum of distant cars was the click of the traffic light beneath which the three of them huddled. The buildings around them were dark.

"All right now," Buddy said, his words barely audible.

"Never be all right . . ." Calvin mumbled.

Shadows moved in an entrance to one of the buildings, people trying to find better ways to sleep on stone, Clay thought. There must be no place in the city where there wouldn't be those shadows, restless, stirring in dark places. He had learned to see them.

Buddy walked on, and Clay hurried to catch up with him. He was shivering so his teeth were clicking like the traffic light. Where were they going to go now?

"Buddy?"

Buddy stopped and turned. "Where's Calvin?" he asked.

A truck rumbled down the street towards them. "Calvin!" Buddy called. He listened for a moment.

"Come on," he said roughly to Clay, and pulled him onto the sidewalk. The truck went by. Clay was dizzy. The truck appeared to be riding on its two left wheels. He sank against a wall. The street was empty except for Buddy standing a few feet away from him, turning in a circle as he continued to call the old man's name. He fell silent a moment, looked up at the sky, then glanced at Clay.

"We got to find a place to get out of the cold," he said.

"Where did Calvin go?" Clay asked, startled by the loudness of his own voice.

"Someplace. I don't know. He'll get drunk. I don't know when or where he'll turn up. If he does. . . ."

"I'm cold," Clay said.

He'd never said until that moment that he was cold

or hungry or scared. Perhaps it was because he had known everyone else was too. But now, the words had fallen from his mouth. He had not been able to stop them.

"You're cold. I'm cold. It's wintertime," Buddy said quickly. "Let's go, little white-neck."

7 Out Cold

They tried the park first. When they got within a block of it, Buddy went ahead to make sure the streets around it were empty. "Stump people gone," he said when he returned. But as they passed the park, they kept across the street from it, close to the buildings.

It was as silent as a cemetery. The streetlight fell on empty benches. Buddy and Clay crossed over and went slowly down the path by the fountain. Clothing, rags, and one rusted eggbeater hung from a tree behind the crate, which was now a low tent-shaped pile of wood. From another tree hung one boot by its laces and Clay's corduroy jacket tied by its sleeves. The straight-backed chair was smashed.

"See? They tried to start a fire in our pail, but it didn't catch," Buddy said, pointing at the pail. "They don't concentrate so good, those people."

"My jacket is on the tree," Clay said.

"Calvin told you to wear all your clothes all the time," Buddy said.

"It got too tight, anyhow," Clay responded.

Buddy went to the tree, jumped up, and pulled the jacket down. The knot had been loose, and the two sleeves waved lazily as the jacket fell. "Never mind tight," Buddy said. "You might need it later."

He said they would go and try the basement windows of the church where they had been given Thanksgiving dinner. The doors would be locked. Everything in the city was locked except the bridges leading out of it, he said, and it was against the law to walk on most of them.

When they came to the church, Buddy went up the stairs and shook the doors. From somewhere above came a ghostly agitated cooing. "Pigeons don't care for their sleep being disturbed," he remarked.

Clay followed him down a narrow passage that ran alongside the church. Every few feet there was a long window close to the ground. When they reached the last one, Buddy put both of his work gloves on his right hand and broke the window with it. "Sorry, church," he whispered. He picked out pieces of glass and piled them neatly nearby. He put his arms around Clay's waist.

"I'm going to drop you through there. Don't stiffen up. Try to land soft," he said.

It felt like a long drop. Clay landed in a crouch, his feet smarting. A second later, Buddy hit the floor with a thump. Clay walked into the sharp edge of a table and felt his way along it until he bumped into a chair that fell with a clatter. He let go of the table, took a few steps, and reached a wall. His fingers touched papers tacked to a cork board. Quickly, he backed to the table. Buddy was saying something he couldn't make out, because of the pounding in his head. He sneezed violently, and the sound of it echoed and reechoed. They must be in a very large room.

Buddy had lit a match and was holding it aloft. Through the broken window came a wave of frigid air as if the night was breathing into it.

"I said, Why are you climbing up on that table, Clay?"

"I thought I could sleep on it," Clay answered. He didn't want to admit he was afraid of the floor, afraid he'd roll into some deep hole and disappear.

"Naw. You'd fall off. They been painting down here. I see some drop cloths in the corner. We'll cover up with them."

A few minutes after Clay had crawled under the cloths, he felt almost warm, although the fumes of paint set off the dizziness that had come over him earlier on the street.

He could hear Buddy close by, snoring faintly. Buddy could always find a place to lie down and sleep. Even if they were at the North Pole, Buddy would make a little house of ice. There'd be a big coal burning inside, and the heat of it would warm every part of him. He blinked at the coal. It blinked back, and he fell asleep.

"Wake up, Clay. Wake up . . ." he heard. It must be so hard to breathe because his head was under the drop cloth. But when Buddy peeled it away, Clay found it was still difficult. There was a fog in his chest. His nostrils felt as if they were stuffed with cotton balls, the kind his mother had kept in a glass jar in the bathroom. He could see that jar with a daisy painted on it. He coughed. He sounded like a dog barking.

"We've got to get out of here before the painters come," Buddy told him.

It was hard to get up. Why not stay where he was? Let the workmen find him. They'd have to take him someplace where he wouldn't need to walk all day long and climb into some hole at night and wake up and be hungry most of the day.

The light was grey and streaky like ink-stained water. He saw now how vast the room was in which they'd spent the night. It came to him suddenly that it was here he had eaten Thanksgiving dinner, probably at that same long table. There were piles of drop cloths everywhere, and mixed in with the smell of paint was the dry powdery smell of plaster. A stepladder stood in a corner. The table he'd wanted to sleep on was the only furniture in the room except for a few folding chairs. The one he'd knocked down last night looked as if it was yawning.

He got shakily to his feet.

"There's a toilet over there behind that door,"

Buddy said, staring at him. "You okay? Your face is red."

"I feel kind of hot," Clay replied. He went off to the toilet. There was a little mirror on the wall. His face *was* red. He washed it with cold water. Wet strands of his hair covered his ears. He hardly knew himself. In the mirror he saw, reflected, the toilet cubicles. He thought of the alleys he'd mostly had to use for bathrooms, anxious and ashamed lest someone see him, and he felt a flash of rage and shame as if some stranger had called him an ugly name.

When he came out, he wandered over to the board he'd touched last night. On one piece of paper was a notice that the parish council would meet Tuesday at 8:00 P.M. to discuss plans for the Christmas pro-gramme and a dinner for the homeless.

Clay was faintly surprised. I can read, he thought.

"Let's go," Buddy said. "Come on. I'll boost you up through the window. We'll go back to the park and see if Calvin turned up."

As they walked back, Clay said, "Gerald might come with breakfast."

Buddy looked down at him distractedly. "I don't know," he murmured. Clay had never heard him sound so sad. Buddy had always set off each morning as though it might be a day of change, a day when his luck would turn.

Under his breath, Clay heard him say, "Monkey Island . . ."

"Why did they come? Why did they howl at us and then break everything up?" Clay asked.

"Nothing inside their heads," Buddy answered. "They got to do something to make sure they're alive. Can you walk faster? We'll have to look for Calvin. He can't take care of himself too well."

Had Buddy been taking care of the three of them? Calvin had once said Buddy was ingenious, and had told Clay to look up the word if he ever got next to a dictionary. Clay thought he knew what it meant.

"Here. I got an apple saved," Buddy said, taking it out of his jacket pocket. "You eat it."

"I'm not hungry," Clay said. He sneezed.

"You're not hungry?" Buddy said. He smiled. "That's a first!"

As dizzy and hot as he was, Clay was relieved that Buddy was friendly again, not the way he'd been last night, so distant and almost cold.

"Maybe there's more left in the park than we saw last night," Buddy said. "We'll go and check it out, and then I'll look in the alleys around, see if Calvin's somewhere, and get back in time in case Gerald comes."

As they passed the drinking fountain, Clay saw Mrs. Crary's paperback books lying among their own scattered pages. Under a bench nearby lay a small pillow with torn lace edges.

"I didn't see Dimp and his dog last night before

those people came," Clay said. He felt tearful, as though he might at any moment burst into sobs.

"Dimp and his dog haven't been around for a week," Buddy said. "What's the matter with you? Losing your memory?"

Clay said nothing because they had reached what remained of the crate.

It looked to Clay like the kind of debris he had often seen on the street, a heap of wood and rags in which you could sometimes find something useful. Then he saw a pair of feet sticking out wearing pink rug slippers. Buddy saw them too. "Oh, God!" he exclaimed, and began to pull everything apart, tossing the split and jagged boards aside as he dug. Beneath it all, lying on his back, his mouth open, was Calvin.

"Is he dead?" Clay asked, his voice trembling.

Buddy was bending over the old man, feeling under his neck. "He's not dead," Buddy said after a minute. "He's out cold." He held up an empty bottle that had been concealed by Calvin's arm. "Rye whisky," he said. "He got hold of this someplace or took it off another drunk. If they want it bad, they can always find it."

Clay heard a moist snort coming out of Calvin's long nose. His beard fluttered slightly.

"I got to get help," Buddy muttered. He stood and looked around. A few cars were passing now, but neither Clay nor Buddy looked in their direction.

"Won't he be all right if he's breathing?" Clay

asked, looking down at Calvin. He willed him to speak, to say anything, even if it was sarcastic. The old man groaned; his legs quivered for a second. He sighed deeply, but he didn't open his eyes.

"You stay here. I'll go see if a phone's working somewhere," Buddy was saying as he looked at a handful of change he'd taken out of a pocket. It was mostly pennies.

Clay sat down next to Calvin and pulled up his knees close to his chest. He was shivering with cold; yet his face felt on fire. "You don't look so good yourself," Buddy said worriedly as he turned to go down the path.

Clay, huddled next to Calvin, didn't move a muscle until the ambulance arrived and drove into the park to within a few feet of the crate. As doors opened, he raised his head. By then, the light had broadened and deepened, a lake of sooty light that had slowly filled up with Clay in the middle of it as still as a stone.

The sound of traffic as it banged and clattered down the streets seemed a continuous echo of a noise inside his skull. He watched the movements of the two ambulance men as though they were taking place in a series of photographs. One lifted Calvin's eyelids with his thumb, took his pulse, felt his slack arms and legs. Both rolled him onto a stretcher, covered him with a blanket, and finally slid him into the ambulance like a coin into a slot.

Buddy touched his shoulder. "You asleep?" he asked.

Clay wasn't sure *what* he was. Everything else was peculiarly distinct, the worn grainy soles of Buddy's shoes as he now knelt to pick through the debris around the destroyed crate, the ripped pages of a book on one of which, after two tries, he made out the word *Crusoe*.

A new photograph was forming: Gerald stepping from a taxi to the sidewalk, carrying two straw baskets and a large thermos bottle.

"What happened here?" he cried out to Buddy as he walked quickly to them. When he was a few feet away, he stopped short and stared at Clay.

"You're a little boy," he said wonderingly, as though it was the first time he'd truly seen him. His mouth widened in his habitual smile that had once reminded Clay of a blind person's, thanking someone for help in crossing a street or avoiding running into a mailbox. It didn't remind him of anything now—any more than Gerald himself did.

"These creeps came last night," Buddy was saying. "Like you see, they tore up the park."

"Where is the old man?" Gerald asked, still looking at Clay.

"On his way to the hospital," Buddy replied. "He got hold of some liquor."

"The others?" Gerald asked.

Buddy shrugged and dropped the slat of wood he

was holding to the ground. How slowly it falls, thought Clay, like a feather. He was so cold except for the burning in his cheeks. He heard Buddy say, "We all ran out of the park. They looked like they wanted to kill somebody."

Gerald lifted the top of the basket and took two doughnuts from it. He held them out.

"Please, take these. This is all so terrible," he said in his gentle voice. "I'll make some telephone calls. I'll protest it, this horrible—" And he looked helplessly at Buddy as though waiting for him to supply the one word that would explain what had happened last night.

Buddy kicked a foot through the heap of rags and wood. "Trash makes trash," he said. Then he took the doughnuts from Gerald's outstretched hands and offered one to Clay. But Clay pushed it away and shook his head.

"The boy is shivering so," Gerald said.

"He's got a bad cold," Buddy said.

"It looks worse to me than a cold."

The cars poured by like metal fragments in a chute.

"He's all right," Buddy said gruffly. "As all right as he can be. I'm going to have to find a place for tonight. Maybe even this afternoon. I'll find somewhere to get him in out of the cold."

The dark would come so early. Clay didn't see how he and Buddy would have time to find a warm hole to crawl into. His shivering was so violent. He felt like a rattle in the hands of a giant baby.

"I think he needs a doctor," Gerald persisted. He looked at Clay closely. "That old man isn't his grandfather, is he? I suppose I knew all along. I didn't wish to think about it."

"His face is awful red," Buddy said with sudden alarm.

Clay rested his head back on his knees. It was almost pleasant to listen to a conversation about himself, though he was so very tired, very sleepy, he found it difficult to follow. Something inside him was loosening like a knot untying itself. He was not going to have to make sense out of this new day. He was glad of that, glad to be free of the strain of it.

He felt himself being lifted up into the air in Buddy's arms. Buddy was saying to Gerald, "The taxis won't stop for me. You'll have to get one and take him."

The strain came back to Clay at once like a weight dropped on his back, pressing the air out of him. "Buddy!" he cried out.

He was held out like a tray, and Gerald took him. It seemed only a second later that he heard a car door opening, and felt himself lowered to a seat. Already the taxi was pulling into the traffic. Clay looked through the window, his head bumping against the glass. Buddy was standing beside the drinking fountain, his arms held loosely at his side, looking off above the cars in the direction of the river. Clay felt tears cooling his burning cheeks. Then the knot inside him untied itself completely, and holding an end of a silky strong rope in each hand, he slipped into darkness.

8 Oxygen

Clay was lying inside a large crib. Through its railing, he glimpsed several other cribs, a white wall, a tall radiator, and a double window that appeared to have been painted black. He puzzled over that. After a moment, he realised it was not black paint but night, and he felt less afraid.

There was a dim light in the room, a dream light. He turned his head in the opposite direction from the window and saw a partly open door, and above it, a bulb upon whose surface he could see dust. Just to the side of the door was a large bulge of scarlet and white. He stared at it until, gradually, it became recognisable. The white was beard and hair, the scarlet was jacket, billowing pants, and tip of nose. It was Santa Claus.

Something pecked the skin of his right hand. He lifted it up, then let it fall back to the bed when he saw it was taped to a thin board and that there was a needle stuck into it. From the needle, a thin transparent tube led up to a bottle that hung by a hook from the top of a metal pole. If he got up and tried to run, the pole and bottle would tag along after him. The picture of it struck him as comical, and he startled himself with a small hoarse laugh.

"You're feeling better," said someone in a low voice. A young woman in a white uniform was standing beside the crib. She smiled down at him. On the top of her head sat a small, pleated round cap like a mushroom.

With his free hand, Clay pointed to the needle, his question asked without words.

"It's full of medicine for what ails you," the nurse said. "What ails you is pneumonia. Your lungs were all filled up, so at first you couldn't breathe well. We gave you oxygen through that thing there by the bed that fits into your nose and makes it easier to breathe. But you don't need it the way you did yesterday when you were brought in." She held up a stethoscope for him to see. "Right now, I want to listen to your lungs."

"What for?" he asked. His voice was thick and blurred.

"Rales," replied the nurse. "To see what those rales are doing."

He didn't have the energy to ask what rales were. Even though he was lying flat on his back, he was very tired. He had been in a hospital once before, when he broke his little finger catching a baseball. His father had taken him to the emergency room. But this time, he was really inside a hospital—maybe the same one where the ambulance had taken Calvin. He didn't actually want to see Calvin now, but thinking about him, especially thinking about Buddy, made Clay feel so sorrowful, his throat ached.

"Don't cry," the nurse said gently, touching his arm above his taped hand. He hadn't known he *was* crying.

"You're going to be fine. You haven't got tuberculosis, or anything hair-raising like that. We're getting rid of all those critters on your head. Your fever has gone down. I'm telling you all this because you must be scared, not sure what happened, and—" She hesitated, smiled, and patted his brow very lightly as though he might break.

He knew what she'd been about to say. Of course he knew. He was alone. A woman had just walked into the room and gone to one of the other cribs. He saw her lean over it. He couldn't see whether the child she was gazing down at so intently was a boy or a girl. It was only a shape under a white coverlet.

He had been brought in by Gerald, a person who hardly knew him.

The nurse would know that. The fact of it would be written down somewhere. Everything was written down, even senseless things.

The nurse said, "In a few days, if you keep improving, a very nice lady from the Child Welfare Association, Mrs. Greg, will come to visit you."

He didn't want to see any Mrs. Greg. *Fee, fie, fo, fum*, he thought to himself. He smelled Social Services—chalky smiles and chalky, dusty words, and people talking importantly over your head.

"Good! No more tears," the nurse noted.

Clay only wanted to see Buddy. He looked directly at the nurse for a moment, at her mushroom hat, her light-coloured eyes. She was looking straight at him too. "Can I touch your cap?" he asked.

She bent over the crib railing until the cap was within reach of his left hand. He ran his fingers along the starched pleats. "Thanks," he said.

"I'm going to put some salve on the sores on your legs," she said, raising her head. "You'll have a lovely deep sleep, and tomorrow you'll feel much better. I promise."

It seemed a long time—after the nurse had gone, after the woman, who had been leaning over the child in the other crib, had clasped shut her big pocketbook and tiptoed out of the room—before Clay felt sleep coming towards him like a warm slow tide that he could draw up over his head like the lightest of blankets.

In the morning, the dusty surface of the window was speckled with flakes of snow that almost at once became watery blotches. A hospital attendant had lowered the railing on Clay's crib, slid a movable table nearly up to his chin, and placed before him a tray holding a bowl of oatmeal, buttered toast, and a small carton of milk.

When he looked at the tray, Clay imagined he'd eat everything up at once. But after a spoonful of oatmeal

95

and a sip of milk, he lay back against the pillow, feeling as though he'd swallowed six boiled potatoes in a hurry.

He did feel better. His right hand was a bit sore where the needle went in, and around it the skin was purplish. He remembered how, when he was little, he used to run away from the doctor when he saw a hypodermic needle in the doctor's hand, and his mother or father would have to bring him back for the shot. Now he had a needle in his hand all the time, and except for the occasional bird-peck pinch, he hardly felt it.

Clay looked across at the only other child in the room, the one whose mother had visited him last night. The railings had been let down on his crib too. Clay realised it was an ordinary bed with railings to keep you from falling off. The boy was sitting up, reading a comic book.

He looked suddenly at Clay and spoke. "I'm going home today," he said. "When are you going home?"

"I've got pneumonia," Clay replied.

The boy nodded and looked wise. "Viral or bacterial?" he asked.

"Just pneumonia," Clay said.

The boy seemed to lose interest in Clay and went back to his comic book, but Clay had a question to ask.

"Is it Christmas?"

"It's only the seventeenth of December," the boy

answered. "You must be really out of it. They stuck that plastic Santa Claus on the wall to cheer us up. You know how they are. I've got haemophilia. That means my blood doesn't clot, in case it's a mystery to you. So I have to get transfusions if I cut myself or have an accident. It's a dangerous life, my father is always saying."

Clay was startled, hearing an actual date, and he said it over to himself several times, *December seventeenth*. But at the boy's subsequent words, he looked at him more closely. He was plumpish with fair smooth skin, and his hair looked newly cut, thick but trimmed around his neck. He was wearing a wristwatch.

"Are you getting better?" Clay asked.

The boy held up his wrist and stared at his watch. Then, as if he had found the answer there, he said matter-of-factly, "I won't get better. It's my hazard."

A nurse carrying a bedpan entered the room and walked towards Clay.

"I can see by your alert expression that you've guessed what this object is," she said. "After you use it, press the button on the cord next to your pillow, and I'll come get it."

She was much older than the night nurse. Clay found her ugly but in a pleasant way, especially when, as now, she grinned at him, showing her big uneven teeth.

The boy was watching. Clay felt embarrassed, much the way he had when he emerged from an alley to find someone smirking at the entrance as though that person knew what he'd been doing. Calvin said it was natural to want to pee in privacy; all animals, human ones too, wanted to except dogs. Some dogs, Calvin claimed, were too jolly and foolish, and too demoralised by their efforts to please everyone, to care about privacy.

The boy spoke. "That's nothing. Everybody has to use one until they can get up on their own and go to the bathroom."

"Thank you, doctor!" the nurse said, bowing to him as she backed out of the room.

Things were taken away, the bedpan, the breakfast tray, a metal wastebasket. Someone came to remake Clay's bed while he lay in a drowse, first on his right side, then on his left as the sheet was snapped and tucked under the mattress. The bottle on the pole was changed. A very tired-looking young woman listened to his chest through her stethoscope. Someone else put salve on his legs. Clay's whole body was warm, even the soles of his feet, a fact that would have astonished him if he hadn't been so sleepy.

He had no idea how much time had passed when he awoke to find the boy in the other bed gone, and to feel his hand clasped by someone else's hand. He turned his head.

"Buddy," he said.

"It's me," Buddy whispered, although there were no other patients in the room.

"You don't have to whisper," Clay said.

Buddy nodded and took a doughnut from the pocket of his jacket, leaving a little trail of powdered sugar across his blue jeans. "Gerald sent you this," he said.

"I'm not so hungry. Could you eat it?" Clay asked.

"It'll help you get strong again," said Buddy.

"I can't," Clay said. "Not yet."

Buddy took a bite from the doughnut. It left a faint trace of white moustache on his upper lip. When Clay smiled, so did Buddy. The snow had stopped. Sunshine lay upon the surface of the window like a pale yellow dust. The room was warm. Clay put his hand on Buddy's arm.

"I've got pneumonia," he said.

"The nurse told me."

"I'll probably have to stay in the hospital ten days. Then the rales will be gone."

"Rales," repeated Buddy.

"They show there's still stuff in your lungs," said Clay.

They looked at each other. Each knew what the other was thinking. What would happen after the ten days? Clay took his hand from Buddy's arm.

"You can't go back on the street," Buddy said. "January is when everything is out to get you. January kills people."

Clay was silent. He couldn't imagine a place beyond

the walls of the room. At the moment, even the floor looked faraway.

"Maybe you'll find your mama now," Buddy said.

Clay couldn't imagine that either.

"I'll never find her," he murmured.

"You can't tell," Buddy said. "In this city, one time, I met a cousin of mine from South Carolina. He's in the navy, and he was walking along West Street. I'd gone down there to look for wood. We met. We couldn't believe it. In a place like this . . . millions of people. You never know."

"What about Calvin?" Clay asked. He couldn't speak of his mother. She had never seemed so absent as at this moment. Soon, Buddy would go. The room felt too warm. His right hand began to ache.

Buddy was looking at him. At least he was still here. Clay noticed how his cheeks gleamed. He must have shaved recently.

"Were you in a shelter?" Clay asked.

Buddy nodded. "I had to find one. It got so cold I didn't think I could make it through the night."

"Calvin?" Clay asked again.

"He's really sick," Buddy said. "All the drinking, all the years. Losing everything. Being lonely."

"Did you get to see him?" Clay asked. "Is he in this hospital?"

"He's in one way downtown. I saw him, but he didn't see me." He took Clay's hand in his own for a moment. "I don't think Calvin's going to make it," he said. "He's too tired."

Clay lay back on the pillow. He and Buddy were silent a few moments. Maybe Calvin was already dead. The strange thing was that, though Clay didn't much like him, he'd cared about him. He'd been interested in the hard, clear way Calvin came out with his thoughts. They weren't like anyone else's. They weren't borrowed thoughts. He wondered if Buddy felt the same way. Buddy had pitied the old man. He must have to have rescued him and taken care of him.

"Are you going to work after you leave me?" Clay asked shyly.

"Oh, yeah," Buddy answered. "Got to have money to do my Christmas shopping." He smiled as though he'd made a good joke. "People don't drink so much soda in the cold weather," he went on. He ate the last bite of doughnut. "I'm thinking about other work, real work," he said. His smile had faded. He just looked worried.

"How's Gerald?" Clay asked.

"He's found a new place down by the river, near where the elevated highway used to be. Lots of homeless down there. Gerald brings them what he can. That's where I saw him this morning."

Clay sat up straight. The needle gave a slight tug at his hand.

"When I'm better, can't we find a place together?" he asked urgently.

"Clay, you are a kid. You've got to have a roof over your head and three meals a day and a school to go to."

"So do you have to have all those things," Clay said.

"It's different for me," Buddy said quickly.

It wasn't different, Clay thought. He closed his eyes. That thick, breathy sleepiness was coming back.

"I think you need to rest now," Buddy said softly. "I'm going to go."

"Will you come back?" asked Clay, opening his eyes with effort.

"If I can," replied Buddy.

On Christmas morning, Buddy came for a brief visit.

"I see they untied you from that tube," he said. "You must be able to walk all over the place." He held out a paper bag. "Here's a present for you."

Inside the bag, Clay found a paperback edition of *Robinson Crusoe*. How many cans had Buddy had to find to lug to a store to get money to buy the book? He could see Buddy was restless, his thoughts elsewhere. When Clay thanked him, he began to pace about the room like the tiger Clay had seen with his father, pacing in his cage.

"I'm getting Christmas dinner at the church," he told Clay. "Remember? Where we had Thanksgiving? I'll be glad when this day is over. I've got things to do."

"Are you still at the shelter?" Clay asked.

Buddy frowned. "Yeah. Nowhere else to be unless I want to freeze."

"What are the things you have to do?"

"I'll tell you when I've done them," Buddy said.

"How's Calvin?"

"He's in a coma. But, you know"—Buddy paused by the bed and shook his head slightly—"they trimmed his beard. I was surprised how young he looks." He clenched his hands a moment. "Clay, I got to go."

Without having to think about it, Clay knew it wasn't a time to plead with Buddy to stay longer, to tell him he'd be glad for his company on Christmas Day. Buddy probably already knew that. He was standing by the door, staring at Clay.

"Okay. See you," Clay said, not quite looking at Buddy's face.

He was gone in an instant.

The ugly, agreeable nurse, Alicia, gave Clay a present too, a small model of a red English double-decker bus. Everything about it was perfect, the tiny spiral stairs, the steering wheel, the rows of seats inside. There were no passengers, no driver.

He held the bus in his hands. Against the thin white coverlet, in the colourless room, the bus was brilliant like a small red comet. One by one, he filled the seats with people—Buddy; Calvin; Mrs. Crary; Dimp Laughlin and his dog; Tony, the boy from the hotel; Gerald; the lady with the turban and the pie; the young man with earrings; Abdul, the news store owner; Mrs. Larkin and Jacob.

After lunch, which was turkey and mashed potatoes and cranberry sauce, he allowed his mother to go up the spiral stairs to the top deck of the bus.

He looked out the window for a while at the grey sky. He took *Robinson Crusoe* from the bedside table and began to read where it fell open in his hands. Then he dropped the book and picked up the bus.

In the front seat on the top deck, he imagined a figure whose coat collar stood up and hid his face. He imagined his mother beginning to hurry towards the figure, thinking it must be his father. Then he shook the bus and everyone fell out of it. Clay picked up the book and began to read at the beginning.

Two days after Christmas, Alicia said to Clay, "Mrs. Greg is coming to see you. You'll like her."

Clay was standing with his back against the window. He wouldn't like Mrs. Greg. He didn't have to.

"And why are you not wearing your slippers?" Alicia asked, pointing to the paper slip-ons beneath the bed.

"They *are* slippers," Clay replied. "They slip right off when I put them on."

"Good point," said Alicia. She pushed a small chair close to the bed and patted the coverlet. "Come on. You're going to be interviewed. It only hurts for a minute." She rolled her eyes. Clay didn't laugh. He was afraid.

Mrs. Greg arrived a few minutes later. She carried a briefcase under one arm and was wearing a thick padded coat that made her look somewhat like a fire hydrant, especially because she was short and, Clay saw when she removed the coat, quite plump. Her eyebrows were two thick pencil strokes, and over her small lips was painted a big bright red mouth.

"Hello, Clay Garrity," she said as she sat down in the chair.

"You're from Social Services," he said.

"Well. So you know all about Social Services. I suppose you can spot one of us a mile away."

"I know you have to sit in Social Services for a hundred years and a day, and then you get papers you fill out so you can come back and sit some more."

Mrs. Greg looked serious. "You're right, Clay. But not entirely. There are so many people in trouble, and not enough money, and not enough really good ideas to make things better. We try to make a very tight net so people won't fall through the way you did. But now we've caught up with you, and you'll be all right."

"What's all right?" he asked angrily, and wished he hadn't. But Mrs. Greg was busy with a notebook and a pencil and seemed not to have noticed his tone of voice. "I have to write things down," she said with a smile. "I forget so easily."

Was she trying to fool him? To show how nice and

easy she was? This won't hurt, the doctor would say, or this will be a bit uncomfortable for a second. And then it *would* hurt like the devil.

"I'd like you to tell me about your life," Mrs. Greg said, her pencil poised above the notebook. "That will help mend that net I was talking about."

He hesitated. He had a superstitious feeling—he told himself it was superstitious—that the more he told her, the greater the distance would grow between himself and Buddy.

Last night, he had been working out how long he'd spent in the park, four weeks and three days. He'd never be able to figure out how many miles he'd walked, going back and forth between the park and the hotel, gathering cans and bottles with Buddy, wandering the streets.

He felt the cleanness of his skin and hair. His sores were healed. He thought of what it would be like to plunge through the net again, back to the iron-grey dirty pavements, the rusty-railed park, the newspapers smelling of urine, the itching and scratching, the gnawing in his belly, the awful grip of loneliness, of being outside of everything.

"My father lost his job," he began. "That was maybe a year ago when his magazine folded. Ma learned to work computers and worked at night. She's having a baby. I guess it's born by now." He glanced quickly at Mrs. Greg, wondering if she knew something he didn't.

106

Mrs. Greg was looking at him attentively, her head cocked slightly forward as though to catch every word.

"Well, my father went away. Missing Persons couldn't find him."

"When do you think that was?" Mrs. Greg interrupted him.

"About seven months ago," Clay replied. "Then Ma stopped working. Pretty soon we couldn't pay the rent. Then we went to the hotel—after Ma went to Social Services. That's where they put us—in that hotel. She went away too. She was gone when I woke up in the morning. I thought she'd come back. She didn't."

"How long ago was that?" Mrs. Greg asked.

"How long have I been in the hospital?"

"Ten days," Mrs. Greg said promptly.

He thought for a moment. "About six weeks and four days," he said. "That's when she went away."

"Someone took care of you in the park? A young black man?"

"Buddy," he said. "And Calvin too. But Calvin drank too much and now he's in a hospital and isn't going to make it."

Mrs. Greg stared at him for at least a minute. He didn't mind. He felt easy now. After all, he'd told her only the truth.

"Do you have relatives anywhere?" she asked at last.

"My father's mother, in Oregon. If she's alive," he replied. "But she won't have anything to do with us."

Mrs. Greg looked very interested.

"Why is that, do you think?" she asked.

"I know why. Because my mother is Italian. And my father's mother said that that ended the family. But my father said she's lost out on everything."

For a second, Clay thought he might start yelling at the top of his lungs instead of speaking so calmly and coolly. Then he recalled what Calvin had said in his dry voice: "Families can let you down." Maybe that was half-true. Calvin had a son he hadn't seen in years, and if Calvin died, the son wouldn't even know he'd left the world. Thinking of Calvin, how funny he could be even when he was sarcastic, made Clay feel less like yelling. "Life is like that," Calvin would have said.

"You must feel you've been dropped from a cliff," Mrs. Greg said softly.

Perhaps he did feel that way. But he didn't want to be told how he felt.

Mrs. Greg was leaning forward. Suddenly she reached out and took his hand. Not quite meaning to, he made a fist, but she kept on holding it.

"Those two men were good to you?" she asked. "They didn't mistreat you?"

"Yes," he answered so loudly they both jumped. "They were so good to me!"

She let go of his hand and glanced down at her

notebook. "Listen, Clay," she began. "You're not going back to the streets. We have to do a few legal things, like making you a ward of the court. That's a formality. And we're going to find you a really nice home with nice people—and very shortly, not in a hundred years and a day. Meanwhile, we're going to look for your parents. I want you to write down your old address and your mother's and father's full names, and where you went to school and the name of the hotel. Also the name of anyone who came to see your mother, like someone from Social Services. All right?"

He thought of Miss You-can't-fool-me. But he wouldn't write *that* down.

"You may find it hard to believe, but your getting sick has a good side to it," said Mrs. Greg. "You can think of this hospital as part of the net."

She isn't so bad, he thought. She probably wouldn't look away from people lying on the sidewalk. She'd probably even worry about them. She had tried hard to understand what it was like for me, squinting her eyes to show me how much she wants to help.

"Okay," he said. He felt older than the small plump woman who was looking at him with so much sympathy on her face. At least, part of him did.

9 The Biddles

Clay's clothes had been washed except for the corduroy jacket. Dirt had worked into it so deeply it was nearly all one colour, an ashy brown. The lining hung from the collar in shreds. He held up a sleeve to his nose. He thought he could smell the trees he had walked on, the ground he had slept on, even the dust-thickened pieces of blanket and canvas he had wrapped himself up in. He bundled up the jacket and held it on his lap, not knowing what to do with it, yet worried at the thought of leaving it in the hospital.

"You look good, Clay," the nurse, Alicia, said on her way to one of the other beds, where she took the temperature of a child with a broken arm, who explained, "My Christmas skates did it."

Clay was sitting on the edge of his bed, waiting. There was a big hole in the sole of his right shoe, but a wad of newspaper Buddy had slipped into the shoe was gone.

He hadn't seen Buddy since Christmas morning. Today was January 2. A new year had begun. He wondered if he would ever see Buddy again. In a paper bag next to him was *Robinson Crusoe* and the English double-decker bus. It was only a toy. Real buses groaned and rumbled along streets, and the drivers in their high seats looked impatient and stony.

"Hello, Clay," somebody said.

A tall, broad-shouldered woman was looking intently at him from just inside the door. She was wearing a thick, fuzzy grey coat. Little wisps of brown hair stuck straight out around her ears from under a black wool hat on her head. She was holding a pair of red mittens and a big black pocketbook in one hand. In the other, she gripped a black jacket.

"I'm Edwina Biddle," the woman said. "I know Mrs. Greg explained to you I'd come to take you home with me today."

She held out the black jacket.

"This is an old thing someone outgrew. But we'll get you a proper coat as soon as we can," she said. "It's very cold outdoors today."

"Thank you," he said. His voice squeaked as though it needed oil.

Alicia smiled at him as she passed the woman on her way to the hall.

"I hope you're hungry. I made a meat loaf for supper, and there's tapioca pudding too."

Clay felt tears spring to his eyes, wash down his cheeks, and touch the edges of his mouth. Edwina Biddle remained near the door. She said nothing but kept a steady gaze on his face. When his tears stopped as quickly as they'd begun, she came to the bed and held out her hands with all the things she was carrying hanging from them. He took hold of them and gave a jump so his shoes smacked the floor.

Later, he was glad she had not rushed over to him and hugged him, or said things like, *Don't cry— everything will be all right*. At that moment, he would not have liked to be hugged by someone he didn't know. He hadn't, after all, been crying because he felt terribly sad or frightened. His tears had come from the burst of relief he had felt at the word *home*.

"I hope you're not married, and I hope you don't smoke cigars," Mr. Biddle said that evening when he arrived home from work. He was a big man, broad in the shoulders like his wife. In his dark brown hair, just over his forehead, grew a startling streak of white hair. Clay smiled politely. Mr. Biddle was a joker.

"Have some gum," he said, holding out the yellow-wrapped stick to Clay. "And call me Henry."

"Don't give him that before supper, Henry," said Mrs. Biddle from the kitchen. "The sugar will take away his appetite."

"Will it?" Henry asked Clay in a serious voice.

Clay shook his head and took the gum.

"You're the strong, silent type, are you?" Henry asked.

Clay coughed.

"I see," Henry Biddle said. He bent over, placed his big hands on Clay's waist, and lifted him straight up in the air. "You don't weigh much," he remarked. "We'll fix that." He held Clay close to him for an instant and set him down on his feet. Clay turned away to hide his smile. He felt there was a reason not to show how much he'd liked being lifted up and held, but he coudn't work out what it was.

"There's a letter from your sister," Mrs. Biddle said to her husband as she came to the kitchen door, "and a rug-sale notice from Macy's, the phone bill, a request to help save the tortoises, seven catalogues, and a mail-o-gram that says you may have won a million dollars. Or was it ten million?"

"You open them and read them," said Henry, hanging up his green storm jacket on a peg in the hall. "Then collect that million and save the tortoises."

Mr. Biddle was a postal clerk and worked all day sorting mail at the post office. Clay could understand why he didn't care to look through mail when he came home.

Mrs. Biddle went back to the kitchen, and Mr. Biddle said, "I'll take a wash and be ready in a jiff."

By then, Clay had seen everything in the apartment, which was on the sixth floor of a seven-storied yellow-brick building on the west side of the city near the river.

The letters were in a pile next to the telephone on a small table in the narrow hallway. Down a few steps

113

and to the right was a living room with a plump sofa and two armchairs, and a round table covered with magazines and a pot of roses. Clay discovered the petals were made of cloth. On one wall hung photographs in silvery-looking frames of children of various ages. A small television set on a metal stand occupied the space between the two windows. On the wall behind the sofa was a large painting of a ship, an old-fashioned kind of ship with four masts and dozens of sails, sitting on a puddinglike blue sea furrowed with neat whitecaps, behind it all a red sun sinking on the horizon. The floor throughout the apartment was covered with peach-coloured carpeting. There were three bedrooms and a bathroom. One of the bedrooms was his. A wall shelf held games and toys, some of which he could tell had been broken and then repaired. On another shelf sat about twenty books, all of which appeared to have been handled and read by many people.

Mrs. Greg had explained to Clay that the Biddles were a foster-parent family. They didn't have children of their own, but they took in other people's children, boys and girls who had no place to live because their parents had died or had gotten too sick to take care of them or, as in his case, had disappeared. Mrs. Greg mentioned that there were other circumstances in which children needed temporary homes, but she didn't go into them. As far as Clay was concerned, she didn't have to. He remembered Tony, his thin, bony, small self huddled up against the hotel wall, his bruised face.

The questions he most wanted to ask but dared not ask yet were about time. Did children stay with the Biddles until they were grown-up? How long would he stay? Would he at some point be sent to another foster family? Would he, one morning, be put out on the sidewalk? He knew this last question was what Calvin would have called wild foolishness. He was connected now, through Mrs. Greg, to Social Services. The net was under him. Still, anything could happen.

They ate supper at a Formica table in the kitchen, where the walls were covered with small framed pictures, a shepherdess watering a sunflower, a rooster crowing on the roof of a barn, two birds holding a wreath in their beaks over the head of a little girl whose chubby hands were crossed in her lap on top of a flounced pink skirt. On several pieces of varnished tree bark were sayings written in such curly letters it was hard to decipher them. *Home Is Where the Heart Is*, Clay spelled out after staring at one while he ate warm meat loaf, peas, and a boiled potato.

He began to feel less strange sitting there. It was as if this real food filling him up so pleasantly was making his first meal with these two large friendly people ordinary as well as unusual. When a green glass bowl filled with tapioca was placed before him, he didn't make a face and growl the way he had when his mother used to urge it on him. Mrs. Biddle handed him a can of evaporated milk with a V-shaped opening and said the tapioca was twice as good with a bit of cream. The food in the hospital had been pale, as if all of it had been boiled for days.

Eating had taken up most of his attention, so he only half listened to the Biddles' conversation. It was mostly about Mr. Biddle's day in the post office, about people who tried to sneak ahead in the line to buy stamps, about his friend, a Mr. Nakashima, who'd found an open envelope addressed to a person and a street that didn't exist, and out of which had dropped an enormous dead spider.

When Clay finished everything, he glanced at the Biddles. They were both smiling at him.

"Good?" asked Mrs. Biddle.

Clay nodded.

"Nice to have you here, Clay," said Henry.

He wanted to smile back at them, but a thought got in the way. Was his old life now blotted out? That was what he'd felt when he'd discovered new people living in the hotel room.

"Thank you," he said.

The next morning, Mrs. Biddle told Clay she would wash the corduroy jacket and reline it. She could see that Clay had long outgrown it.

Clay imagined a boy somewhere in the city at the very moment of being lost, and set on a path that would lead him through hard days and nights to Edwina Biddle's apartment, where Clay's old jacket, spruced up, would be waiting for him in a closet.

They went to shop on Broadway. Mrs. Biddle bought him two pairs of shoes, sneakers and brown oxfords, blue jeans and two pairs of corduroy pants, a sweater, three shirts, socks and underwear, a navy blue down jacket and a wool hat, a toothbrush, and a canvas bag for schoolbooks.

"That's a nice belt for you," she said, pointing to one curled on a counter, a silver eagle emblazoned on its buckle. He ran a finger over the eagle, feeling its taut wings stretched in flight.

"Would you like it?"

"Thank you. Yes, Mrs. Biddle."

"Call me Edwina," she said. "I'd love that."

After supper, Henry cut his hair. When Clay went to look in the bathroom mirror, he didn't look familiar to himself. Of course, he was taller. It was odd to think he'd been growing all the time he'd lived with Buddy and Calvin in the park. His face was very thin. His brown eyes stared into their own reflection. Did he really look like his father, as his mother had often remarked? What did his father look like?

The school he was to attend was a ten-minute walk from the Biddle apartment. After he took reading and arithmetic tests, he was placed in one of the four sixth-grade classes. His homeroom teacher, Miss Moffa, called him Charles for several days. In the end, she got his name right but didn't pay much attention to him. He could see she had her hands full keeping the class quiet enough to give out assignments.

He was the thirty-third student in his class. His desk was next to a girl who, as soon as he sat down, gathered up her pen and pencils and a blue comb and moved them all away as though she knew he meant to grab them.

He had been worried the first day he'd entered the old grey stone building with its great dirty windows. A man in uniform had passed a device like a ray gun over him and the other children to make sure no one was carrying a concealed weapon.

But nobody bothered him much. During class changes, the corridors were packed. Some of the bigger boys and girls punched anyone they could reach with their jabbing fists. There was one who cursed and screeched with laughter whenever he landed a blow. His face was bone white, and bristles of hair stood up on his scalp like porcupine quills. Clay named him Son of Stump People.

In a week, he had made a friend. His name was Earl Thickens. His smile reminded Clay of Buddy's. They ate lunch at the same table in the school cafeteria. Whenever there was a free period, they sat together. Neither Earl nor he asked each other about their families.

"Don't let anyone see your belt with that eagle on it," Earl advised him. "Somebody will take it off you."

In the afternoons especially, the school was a crazy

house of noise. There was fighting in the corridor, bells clanged, teachers shouted to try and bring about order. Clay set himself against it all. He discovered he wanted to read anything he could get his hands on, to learn everything.

When he couldn't hear the teachers' voices through the din, he watched their lips. In time, he got pretty good at guessing what they were saying. He wrote it all down and did his homework regularly. Sometimes he could escape into the library, which smelled of paste and dust and books, and where it was quiet like a cove you could row your boat into to get out of the gale wind.

In the long-ago days when he'd lived with his father and mother, a teacher had written on his home report that he daydreamed too much.

He didn't daydream any more. He remembered.

One bitter afternoon in late January when the wind blew fiercely through the streets and rattled signs and doors, he went downtown with Earl to a store that sold old comic books. While Earl went through stacks of *Spider Man* comics, Clay stared through the store window at the street. It had begun to look familiar. His gaze fell upon the entrance to an alley that ran alongside a big apartment house.

It was where he and Buddy had found a hoard of bottles and cans to redeem. He realised with a shock that made his knees quake that he couldn't be more than a few minutes' walk from the park.

Earl shook his arm. "Hey! You going into a trance?"

"I was thinking about something."

"Think on this," Earl said, holding an open comic book in front of Clay's face. With one finger, he pointed to a vampire that seemed to have been drawn with black shoe polish except for her gruesome white fangs.

"Doesn't she remind you of Miss Moffa?" Earl asked. "Especially when it's teacher vampire hour at three PM?"

"She's prettier," Clay said. Earl laughed.

Monkey Island, Clay was hearing, *where the monkeys live*. In his mind's eye, he could see those bawling faces, those bodies hauling themselves along, coming towards the park, set on damage and hurting, worse than any shoe polish vampire or irritable teacher.

Earl was paying the clerk for the comic book. He made a little money on weekends putting fliers in mailboxes for a Chinese take-out restaurant. Edwina often asked Clay if he needed a dollar or two. But he didn't care much for comic books, and he couldn't think of what else he wanted. He did like the newspaper Henry brought home every evening. He read it all through, sometimes even the apartment ads.

"You want to do something?" Earl asked when they were out on the sidewalk. "Like go down to the river and those old warehouses? Or we could go to where they're putting up that new office building and look through the holes in the fence."

"It's too cold for the river," Clay said.

"Well—what *do* you want to do?" Earl asked a little crankily. "You're all wrapped up like a package today."

"There's a place near here . . . if you want to come with me," Clay said, not sure he really wanted Earl along.

Earl shrugged and thrust the comic book into a pocket. "Let's go," he said.

There were a number of streets to choose from. Clay made several false starts until suddenly his memory shaped itself into an arrow. He headed down a broad avenue.

"Bird-dogging," remarked Earl. "What's the mystery?"

Clay was unable to speak. Not much more than fifteen minutes from the comic-book store, the avenue split in two to fork around the triangular park.

For a second, Clay felt so dizzy he thought he would pitch forward to the street. He grabbed Earl's arm. There were no newspapers along the paths, no black plastic sacks. The cement drinking fountain had been removed. One bench, most of its slats broken, stood on its three remaining legs under a tree.

The park was only a pause in the streets, a small place surrounded by rusty iron rails where trees had trouble staying alive.

"What are we looking at?" asked Earl.

"I lived there for five weeks," Clay said, letting go of Earl's arm. "In that park, over in that far corner, in a kind of crate house."

He stared at the corner, seeing himself in the big sweater Buddy had found for him, sitting at the entrance to the crate, looking up to see what Buddy was going to take out of a pocket or a paper bag for them to eat.

"You were on the street," Earl stated.

"Yes."

Earl blew on his fingers, looking over them at Clay.

"My cousin, Lawrence, is on the street," he said. "He sleeps over to the Port Authority except when the cops chase him away. We haven't got room for him. My mother takes him food when she can."

Earl went far out of his way to walk Clay almost to the Biddle apartment. It was still hard for Clay to think of it as home, but on this dark, cold afternoon, after seeing the park, it wasn't possible at all.

He was silent at supper that night. He knew he was making the Biddles uncomfortable. Henry told jokes. Edwina piled food on his plate. He couldn't do what they wanted, laugh at Henry's stories or tell them about school, or about what Earl and he had done that day. It wasn't the first time he'd felt their disappointment.

He did the chores he was asked to do, made his bed, dried dishes, helped to clean the apartment on

Saturday mornings, put his soiled clothes in the hamper for Edwina to take to the Laundromat down the block. But they wanted more from him, even though Edwina told him he was the easiest boy she had ever taken care of. As she spoke, there was a questioning note in her voice as if she hoped he would contradict her.

It flashed into his mind that she might be relieved if he acted up a little, balked at a chore for once, sulked and slammed shut his bedroom door.

This sense, this knowledge, of what grown-ups were feeling was new in Clay. He thought it had come to him because he had lived like a grown-up himself all those weeks.

It wasn't that Buddy and Calvin hadn't known he was a child. But in some deep way, he'd been on his own. He'd been one of them.

It filled him with a somewhat spooky hilarity to realise that he had real thoughts of his own. From the time you learned to talk, he thought, people were always saying, *Think about what you're doing! Don't be thoughtless!*

One of his thoughts was that people only saw you when you were standing in front of them. By now, the nurse, Alicia, would have had many more patients. Mrs. Greg would have seen and tried to help many more children in trouble. And if he suddenly disappeared, the Biddles would take in a new boy or girl. Henry would make jokes to get them to smile.

Edwina, in her kindly way, would see that their socks were clean and that they had warm sweaters. But Clay did make an effort now and then to talk to them more than he felt like talking.

He felt his mind had become a clean, bare room with a hard, clear light shining in the centre of it.

He did pretty well in school. He kept away from the really rough kids. There was nothing he wanted from them. He knew most of the places where drugs were dealt and used, and he avoided them. He and Earl learned a large part of the city like a lesson in a book.

The truth was simple. He was alone. His father had left. His mother had left. In time, he'd grow up and find a job and have a small apartment of his own and take care of himself. Nothing lasted forever.

But there was one shadowed corner in the bare, clean room of his mind. In that shadow, he glimpsed Buddy standing motionless, looking at him gravely, and he felt an enormous longing to see him, and an uncertainty about all these new thoughts that had come to him with his trouble.

In early March, there was a blizzard, and school shut down for two days. The whole city seemed to have shut down. There was hardly any traffic. Only a few people moved about the streets, thickly muffled in clothing, their heads down.

Clay kept to his new routine. In the afternoon, he

went to the park. It took him just under forty-five minutes to reach it. When he got there, he walked all around the railing before going up the path to the corner. He'd been doing this on the afternoons he didn't spend with Earl, even on weekends when he'd finished whatever he had to do at the Biddles'.

Nearly two feet of snow had fallen. The traffic light clicked, but no cars passed. His were the only tracks in the drifts that had piled up along the paths. On the sidewalk, in front of the big building on the far side, a man with a long scarf wrapped around his head and face trudged through the snow as lights went on above him in several windows. It was so silent, as silent as it might have been in a forest of great trees.

What had happened to Mrs. Crary? To Dimp Laughlin and his dog? To the boy with the earrings? Calvin was probably dead. But Buddy couldn't be dead.

What am I doing here? Clay asked himself, and answered, I'm looking for Buddy.

He let himself into the apartment with his key. He heard voices from the living room, Edwina's and someone else's that was vaguely familiar. After he'd hung up his jacket, he looked into the room and saw Mrs. Greg sitting in an armchair, taking a sip from a cup of tea. She smiled at Clay.

"Here he is!" she cried.

Edwina said, "Oh, Clay! I was getting worried. Did you and Earl go off somewhere? It's already dark."

125

"I walked in the snow," Clay replied, staring at Mrs. Greg.

"Mrs. Greg has something grand to tell you," Edwina said, and her voice trembled very faintly.

"Clay," Mrs. Greg began. He held his breath. "We've found your mother and your tiny new sister."

"Lucy?" he said so quickly he didn't think either of them heard him gasp.

"Her name is Sophie, actually," said Mrs. Greg. "She looks quite a bit like you, Clay. Your mother is living in a shelter with other women and their children. She'll be moving into a place of her own very shortly. And then you'll be with her. She was so happy to know you were safe and being taken care of. Yes. We made the connection—it's truly wonderful how it all came out—just patient work," and at this point, Mrs. Greg appeared to ponder on how wonderful it all was.

Wonderful didn't fit Clay's feeling at that moment, unless it could mean dazed, unless it meant the faint hollowness he had often felt when he woke up bundled in rags and canvas, hearing old Calvin snoring a foot away, or else Buddy breathing lightly as though he were never fully asleep.

He felt a strange embarrassment too, as though he was waiting for a huge sensation of surprise that was somehow passing him by.

Then he thought—I have a sister, Sophie, and he was able to smile at Mrs. Greg.

"Well! I should say!" she exclaimed, smiling back at him. "Tomorrow I'll come and get you after school, and I'll take you to her. I know how eager you must be. . . ."

He nodded energetically, hoping the two women would not notice his silence.

Edwina said, "Clay, I'm so glad for you."

That night at supper, Henry didn't make a joke. He said what a miracle it was that people could find each other even in this vast city, that things can turn out fine. Looking at Clay and touching his arm, he said, "We're going to miss you when you move in with your mom. But you'll come and visit us sometimes? Many of the children do, for a while."

"Yes," Clay croaked. It was hard to talk. Whenever he meant to agree with Henry, to say how glad he was his mother had been found, an opposite feeling would push up behind his words. But it wasn't that he was not glad. It was rather that he couldn't understand at all why the small explosions of joy that rose up in him became muted at once as if they couldn't make their way through a dense cloud of bewilderment and discontent.

The women's shelter was an old brick house on the Upper West Side of the city. When Clay looked up at it and caught sight of a woman passing in front of a bay window, carrying a child, he pulled away from Mrs. Greg.

"Clay, what is it?" she asked.

He shut his mouth tightly so nothing could come out of it that would surprise them both. The big glass doors opened. He found himself in a large, disordered room full of worn furniture, toys, and children's clothes folded and piled up on chairs as though just taken from a dryer. Unframed pictures of babies were taped to the walls. A young woman with long black hair was sitting on a couch, nursing an infant. Clay looked quickly away. Mrs. Greg was speaking with a thin, tall woman wearing steel-rimmed eyeglasses who glanced at Clay from time to time. She beckoned to him, and when he went to stand beside her, she looked at him gravely as she stroked his hair.

"Your mother is in her room," he said. "We'll go up. She's been expecting you all day."

"I was in school," he said.

"Oh, she knew that."

They walked up a broad, curving, uncarpeted staircase. The banister was shaky. He heard babies crying, a child shouting, "Waffles, Mama!" and the rise and fall, like wavelets, of women's voices. The lady with the glasses pushed open a door that was already ajar.

On a narrow bed sat Clay's mother. Next to her on a white flannel cloth was a sleeping infant.

She and Clay looked at each other. He glanced behind him. Mrs. Greg and the woman with the glasses had withdrawn into the hall and were speaking together softly.

His mother held out her arms.

He took two steps. Her hair was short, cropped like a little cap around her head. She was thin. When he had imagined her all these weeks, she had been heavy, carrying the baby that now lay outside of her on the bed.

"Clay," she whispered.

He went up to her, felt her arms around his shoulders, and was startled when she let fall the whole weight of her head against his neck.

He was speechless. She kissed his cheeks and his forehead. He looked at the baby. Her face was as quiet as a small pond. She frowned slightly; a faint tremulous smile twitched her lips. For an instant, her hands moved like birds fluttering.

"Clay," said his mother again, pushing the hair from his brow. "You're parting your hair. You look so grown-up. You have grown. Oh, Clay. I've missed you so."

"You went away," he managed to say. It was not what he'd meant to say, although what that was, he wasn't sure.

His mother bowed her head and stared at the baby. He could hear everyone breathing, his mother, the baby, himself. Then she looked directly at him and began to speak quickly as though she'd said the words she was now saying many times before to herself.

"I think I was out of my mind," she said. "I couldn't go back to that place. I'd left the money for you under the doughnuts—did you find it?—so I must have known I wasn't coming back. I wandered the streets. I was frightened of what I was doing—leaving you like that. But I couldn't go back there. And I thought—God knows if I thought at all—that somehow you'd be taken better care of if I wasn't there."

She paused. Her face was close to his and it was flushed all the way to her forehead. He saw she felt shame. Some of it poured out of her and touched him and so he felt it too, for both of them, for what had happened to them.

"I don't know how to explain it," she went on. "All I could think about was getting away. It's more than you should have to take in, but that's the truth of it. I fell apart. The night I left, I slept in a doorway. I panicked in the morning, thinking about the baby, thinking I'd lose it, that I had to do something. I tried to talk to a woman on the street. I couldn't speak. It was as if language had been taken from me. Then another woman at Pennsylvania Station took hold of me, actually grabbed my arms and led me to this place. I couldn't speak, Clay. I couldn't write down words on paper for people to read. I was locked in. Then the baby came just over three weeks ago. I heard her first crying. And I was able to talk then. Our social worker, the one who tries to help us here, took down everything about you and where we'd been, everything. And they found you. And that's what happened."

The baby awoke. Her eyes were blue.

"Their eyes are always blue in the beginning," his mother said. "Sophie," she murmured, and picked up the baby and cradled her in her arms.

"I'm all right now, Clay. In a few weeks or a month, there'll be an apartment ready for us, all of us," she said.

"Daddy?" he asked quickly.

"No," she answered sombrely. "But I know he's alive. If he wasn't, I'd have heard. We can hope he'll come back. I think now that maybe the same thing happened to him that happened to me. But we can manage. In a few months, I'll put the baby in day-care. I'll get a job, only this time it will be a day job."

He touched the baby's cheek. She had fallen asleep again. He touched her ear.

"Clay, I know you can't forgive me. Did Mrs. Larkin help you? I thought she might. She knows her way around all these agencies."

"She gave me soup," he said.

His mother groaned. "It all happened," she said as though she couldn't believe it. She put Sophie back on the white flannel cloth and looked down at her. Clay hoped the baby would wake. He wanted to hear her voice.

"You suffered," his mother said in so low a voice, he had to lean forward to hear her. "I know you did. I thought about it all the time, and about Daddy going away. If saying sorry was enough, there'd be no hard feelings in the world. I am sorry, but what can you do with that? They told me how you lived—like a stray animal, and then sick and alone in the hospital. Sorry can't erase all that. There must be a way for people to go on caring for each other that's a long way beyond *sorry*." She looked up at him and smiled hesitantly.

He looked away from her smile. He had listened to what she'd said, but he coudn't think about it yet. She hadn't been there at all; now there was almost too much of her.

"You don't have to forgive me," she said. "I can bear that. But you'll have to get to a place beyond forgiveness. . . ."

The baby woke then with a small but piercing cry.

10 Searching, Finding

On a Saturday morning at the beginning of April, Clay stood at the door of a small apartment in a building on a street two subway stops south of the Biddles' apartment. Beside him was a shopping bag containing his clothes, the red double-decker bus, and the copy of *Robinson Crusoe* Buddy had given him. The canvas bag that held his schoolbooks hung from one shoulder.

"Welcome home," his mother said. She had been putting groceries away, and she was still holding a carton of milk. When she hugged him, he felt the coldness of the milk through his sleeve.

Sophie was lying on her back on a small sofa. When his mother had released him, he went to look at her. She seemed interested in the ceiling.

"She'll recognise you soon," his mother said, putting a can of tomato sauce on a shelf. The kitchen was so small, he could see most of it through the doorway. When he looked back down at Sophie, her eyes were closed.

Edwina had planned to bring him to the new

apartment. For the first time since he had gone to live with the Biddles, he had argued with her. He wanted to go to his mother by himself. He had grabbed Edwina's hand and kept hold of it. She gave in to him at once, looking down at his hands clasping hers. He realised it was the first time he had really touched her.

"But you must call me when you get there," she had said.

"I will," he promised.

"I'd like to see the baby," she said.

"Oh, you will," he said. His foster parents and his mother would meet, he knew, but there was a part of him that wished he could leave the Biddles and not see them again. It was the same part of him that was reluctant to return to the triangular park; yet he continued to go there whenever he had the time.

His mother had come to look at Sophie. "She'll sleep for a while," she said. She held out her hand to Clay. "I'll show you everything."

She smelled soapy, fresh, new, like everything in the apartment. He tried to think of her that way, part of the varnished floor of the living room, the standing lamp whose base was still wrapped in cardboard, the three small cabinets in the kitchen glistening with white paint.

The baby's crib was next to her bed in a room that was only large enough for one other piece of furniture, a small chest of drawers. There was beige tile in the bathroom, and a powdery new shower curtain that smelled chemical. In an alcove off the living room was a single bed covered with a blue blanket, and two long shelves for his books and clothes. "We'll get a chest for you as soon as I start a job," she said. He put the bus and his books on one shelf. His mother was taking his clothes from the shopping bag, folding them, and placing them on the other.

"The Biddles bought you these," she said. She sighed. He knew she was thinking that she ought to have gotten him the clothes. He had a sudden picture of her huddled in a doorway. She wasn't new, any more than he was.

"There are such angels in the world," she said. He was startled, recalling the conversation about saints between Buddy and Calvin.

"They get paid by Social Services," he said.

His mother looked at him thoughtfully. "Even angels have to make a living," she said.

"I have to call Edwina," he said.

She took him to the window in the living room, where she pointed across the street to a telephone booth. 'We'll get a phone in a week or so," she said. "I'll watch you from here. Do you have a quarter?"

"I have one," he said. "You don't have to watch me. I go everywhere by myself."

"I know that," she said. "I'd just like to."

When she answered the phone, Edwina said, "Now you're really home."

At her words, he felt a stab of irritation. He didn't

want anyone to tell him where he was. Quickly, he described the apartment. "Even the stove and refrigerator are new," he said. "And the halls aren't marked up yet with anything, not even in the elevator."

Then, because he felt faintly ashamed of something he'd said to his mother, he couldn't remember what, or because Edwina's words about home had bothered him, he said, "My mother says you're angels."

Edwina laughed. "Well, I must tell Henry at once. Until now, he's not been sanctified."

When he left the booth, he looked up at the apartment house. At a window on the fourth floor, his mother stood holding Sophie, smiling down at him. He had an impulse to wave. Instead, he put his hand in his pocket and went across the street with his head down.

Clay was able to attend the same school, although he had told himself he wouldn't have been surprised if he'd been transferred to another. He had made himself ready for that possibility by not hoping for anything. Still, he was very glad there'd been no transfer, mostly because of Earl, and because of the new librarian, Miss Sanders. "A new book came in I think you'd like," she would say, looking at him seriously. And a week ago, she suggested he take home *David Copperfield*. "You're ready for it," she'd said. "It'll wither your timbers."

It was the beginning of May, and the breeze that

blew down the streets along which Clay walked to school no longer had the sky smell of winter. Chicken roasting in the take-out place, whiffs of chemicals from the dry cleaner's, the exhaust from buses and cars, and the faint citrus aroma of the grapefruit and oranges in their crates at the entrance to the fruit and vegetable markets, gave a human smell to the air. A few stunted trees planted in squares of earth at the edge of the sidewalk, their lower trunks surrounded by chicken wire, were veiled in green, with their new leaves the colour of pea pods.

Clay's mother had found a job two weeks earlier in an insurance office, and Sophie spent the day, until 4:00 PM, with a young woman who lived on the floor above their apartment and who had two small children of her own. On weekends, Earl and Clay went to the places they liked, the comic-book store, the warehouse district, new building sites, and one they'd recently discovered, a promenade right on the Hudson River where boats were moored, bobbing on the water, their sails furled tight as the new leaves.

But at least once a week, Clay went back to the park. He suspected that someday soon, he would give up the park. He had given up hope of finding Buddy.

And then on a Friday afternoon at the end of the first week in May, he found him.

He had been standing beside the tree that was next to where Calvin's crate had been. It was late in the day, but the air was still warm, and there was a thin

buttery light that softened the stony façades of buildings like a transparent yellow cloth hung over them.
There were three new benches. On one of them sat an
elderly man reading a newspaper. His shoes were
shined, and he wore a light topcoat. A boy on a
skateboard suddenly shot by on the path near where
Clay was standing. A woman with a small, plump,
white-furred dog on a long leash walked slowly the
length of the park.

Clay had turned to look at a building that had been
dark and empty when he had lived in the park. Now it
had many curtained windows. Out of the corner of his
eye, he saw a man on a bicycle waiting for the light to
change at the corner. The man was looking at the park.
His eyes suddenly fixed on Clay. He held up his arms
to the sky, the bicycle started to topple, he leapt from
it, dragged it to the sidewalk, and began to run just as
Clay did.

They met at the iron railing.

"Where have we *been*!" Buddy exclaimed, leaning
over and grabbing Clay's shoulders. "I've been thinking and thinking about you! Every time I ride by here,
I see little Clay in his corduroy jacket, and I say to
myself, where *is* he? And now look at this. You're
here!"

Clay was laughing, hanging on to Buddy's arms.
"I've been coming here for months, thinking
maybe—and now you're here too!" he cried.

Buddy wore dark blue running shoes and a lightweight beige jacket. He was shaved close to his skin, and although the bicycle didn't look new, it was in good shape.

"Who goes first? You or me?" asked Buddy.

"You," said Clay.

Buddy, smiling, climbed over the railing, and Clay leaned against him. Buddy placed his hand on Clay's head the way he used to do. For a moment, they stood there like that. "Got to keep my eye on my wheels," Buddy said, turning back to the railing. They both leaned on it.

"Okay, here goes," Buddy said. "I stayed in a shelter, had to—the weather would've killed me. I hated that place. . . . Well, I had nothing left for anybody to steal. I do now. My shoes, my jacket, my clean shirts. I found a new shelter with strong lockers. That was after I got a job. Messenger. It's a Wall Street office—firm, they like to call it. I carry stuff all over the city, papers, letters, and like that. I was always good on a bike. I could take it upside of a building, you know, Clay. And I started high school, night classes. I'm fixed up. Beginning to be. I've saved eight hundred fourteen dollars. When I get a thousand, I'm going to get a place of my own. Queens, maybe. You have to have the deposit and two months' rent. Nobody's giving you anything. When I get the high school certificate and the place, I'll see what to do next. I have plans. But I won't speak about them yet. There's no telling."

"You didn't come back to the hospital again," Clay said with a touch of shyness.

"I knew you were going to be all right," Buddy said. "I couldn't come back. Too much on my mind."

"What happened to Calvin?" Clay asked.

"He died," Buddy said, and shook his head. "He was too sick. There wasn't anybody or anything for him. I went to see him the last few days he lived. For about an hour, he came to and could talk. He asked about you—said, 'Did that boy find his mother?'"

"Yes," said Clay, feeling he was telling it to both Buddy and Calvin. "I found her. Or Social Services did. I have a new sister. Sophie. My mother has a job, and we live in an apartment. I'm going to school. I can walk there from home."

"Home. That's good," said Buddy.

The word had slipped out. Clay thought about it. He couldn't take it back. That would mean trying to explain the tangle of feelings he had about his mother and his father—and home. The tangle was something inside him, alive and mysterious. When he'd said *home* just now, it seemed for a moment that everything in his life was clear, that the tangle had disappeared.

"You hear anything about your daddy?" Buddy was asking.

Clay shook his head. "We don't know where he is," he said, "but he's not dead."

They stared at each other, both thinking, perhaps, of

the huge country into which Clay's father had disappeared, a country like an ocean.

"You remember the night the stump people came to beat us up?" Clay asked. "That's what Calvin called them—stumps."

"I'm not likely to forget them," Buddy replied.

"Maybe Calvin wouldn't have died—" Clay began, but Buddy interrupted him.

"He would have anyhow."

"Maybe they made it happen sooner," insisted Clay.

"Maybe, but I don't think so. Something would have made him want liquor—a car banging into another car, a fight in the park."

"They called you that word," Clay said.

"Yeah," said Buddy. "It wasn't the first time, won't be the last."

"If they said they were sorry, would you have forgiven them?"

Buddy laughed aloud. "Forgive them! They're just part of the sludge I got to make my way through. If a snake bit you, would you forgive it? It's what snakes do. It's what people like that do. Sorry is nice but short. *Nigger* is the longest word I know."

"What's a place beyond forgiveness?" he asked Buddy urgently.

"Your own room," Buddy said. "You have to go your own way."

"Can we see each other again?" asked Clay.

"When I get a permanent address," Buddy replied. He took a pencil and a slip of paper from a jacket pocket. "Write down your phone number," he told Clay.

Clay wrote it down and, next to it, wrote his full name.

"It may be a while," Buddy said. "But you know I've got you in my mind. Now I've got to go a ways from here for a pickup. I'm truly glad you and your mother found each other. You're lucky, one of the lucky ones. You know that, don't you, Clay?"

Clay nodded because Buddy had said it. The truth was he hadn't thought about luck.

On his way home, he remembered Calvin's notebooks, and what he'd told Clay he'd been writing down—a history of his life and times. When the park was cleaned out, someone must have thrown Calvin's notebooks into the back of a garbage truck.

Perhaps the old man had simply liked writing things down, part of his staying neat in a cyclone. Clay smiled, imagining himself trying to tie his shoelaces and comb his hair as hurricane winds blew houses and trees past him. It made him think of Charlie Chaplin.

His father had taken him once to see an old-fashioned movie. Clay recalled a scene where a blizzard was roaring around a tiny cabin perched on the edge of a cliff. Inside the cabin, Charlie had set out a dining place for himself at a rickety table, and with very delicate manners, was eating a plateful of shoe-laces as though it were spaghetti. He'd like to see that movie again.

When he saw his apartment house ahead, he began to run towards it.

He opened the door with his key. His mother was sitting on the couch, resting, her head back. A foot away, Sophie was asleep in her stroller. His mother must have just brought her home from her day-care upstairs.

"Ma," he called, louder than he'd meant to. She started and looked at him. He went to her and touched her arm that lay along the arm of the couch.

"I was lucky," he said. "We were all lucky."

"Yes," she said.

There was a sudden cry.

He turned. The baby was looking right at him, her hands flying towards him, her eyes bright with recognition.

"Oh, Sophie!" Clay said.